Shears of Fate

Alexandria V. Nolan
Copyright © 2012 Alexandria Nolan

All rights reserved.

ISBN-13:
978-0615897172

ACKNOWLEDGMENTS

For anyone who has ever lost part of
themselves. I hope that you rediscovered it--or
put it to rest.

For my mother, who listened patiently to all of
my ideas.

For my father who first told me the stories of
the asylum.

and as always, all that I do is for TJN.

ALEXANDRIA NOLAN

Those who have been indulged by fortune and have always thought of calamity as what happens to others, feel a blind incredulous rage at the reversal of their lot, and half believe that their wild cries will alter the course of the storm.

GEORGE ELIOT

ALEXANDRIA NOLAN

Journal

January 18, 1935

My best friend Violet was beaten, raped and left for dead. It happened on a crisp October day, one of the few we didn't spend together. Am I shocking? My apologies, but I wanted the facts to be understood right from the beginning. I hate the stories one reads wherein one feels an affinity with a character, and then the author kills them off in the end. That type of disappointment and sadness has no place here. Violet couldn't stand those types of stories either. She'd throw a book down in disgust if it started going that way.

You see, the doctors say that if I am ever going to get over this, that I ought to write about Violet. My doctor has also encouraged me to write about my changing moods, memories, and feelings. I'm not as certain about that, but perhaps they're right. I can't think I'll have much to write about here in the asylum if the days keep passing the way they have been...truth be told there isn't a whole lot to write about. What I do know is that I am tired of Violet being labeled as a victim. I hate hearing about her as "Violet David, the girl that got raped". If she was around and heard that, she'd punch someone right in their fat face. That was the kind of girl she was.

If the doctors here think it will "cure" me to write, I'll write. I'll tell you what Violet was like. Because it's not fair that she can't just be known for herself, but instead has been turned into this tragic character that she would have hated. Before the story of what happened to her was as stuck to her as her cold, bruised skin. If you would have known her, you would have liked her. Everyone did. You couldn't help it. She was alive and bossy and difficult and loud and always laughing. That's the girl I want you to meet. And since you can't, I'll try to introduce her the only way I know how.

Hopefully, whatever I find to fill these pages will satisfy these doctors. Perhaps once they get together and really see her the way they ought to, they'll let me out of this asylum. Maybe, I won't miss her so much. Maybe.

Letter from Alice David to her brother, Arthur

January 6, 1935

Dearest Artie,

Ever since that day in October, I scarcely know myself. I'm not the wife I used to be, I'm not the mother. The visits are getting more and more difficult. I can't tell you how much I miss Violet, and how Max and I would do anything to bring her back. She seems farther away than ever.

The doctors here at the State Hospital are trying a few experimental therapies, but no one has any answers. It's terrifying to see her face and hear her stories. Haunting and heartbreaking. As if Violet's tragedy wasn't enough, the experience of the asylum is enough to break anyone. Sometimes I can't understand how anyone could hope to be cured in such a place. I fear that my faculties are failing me. I am over-exhausted and need rest. Please write me a cheerful note to lift my spirits and give me strength.

All my love to your family,

Alice

Journal

January 20, 1935

Violet's parents came to visit me today. My own parents are back in Chicago, and Mrs. David is kind enough to correspond with them on my "condition". It's always awkward when she comes to visit, Mr. David is nice enough, and warm, but I always have the feeling that Mrs. David doesn't like me. Sometimes I think she blames me for what happened, or even that she wishes it was me instead of Violet. I can hardly blame her.

No, the most interesting thing about me is that I was close to Violet. I was a mousey little nobody compared to her. Even now, I owe my relative comfort to her. Even now that she's gone, I am better from just knowing her. We used to always come up here to Traverse City, to stay at her parent's Lake Michigan house. And so, now, after the breakdown, everyone thought it was best that I was brought up here to the State Hospital for treatment. Away from Chicago, away from where it all happened. Away from any negative memories.

But, they were the crazy ones if they thought my location would matter. Violet is with me always. We were more than best friends, we were like sisters, like two halves of a whole. But, since I don't care much where I am, Traverse City is no better or worse than anywhere else.

We'd come up here summers and flirt with the local boys. Buy some caramels, wade in the Lake. We both loved Chicago, but the small town of Traverse City was always wilder, and made us both more fierce and independent. It was also a treat to escape from the smothering Chicago heat. The wind coming off the Lake would find us both, arms outstretched, hair blowing back, smiles stuck to our faces. Those were beautiful days. We grew from awkward little girls, knobby knees and jutting elbows to young women. Ready to be adored, fallen in love with and kissed regularly. How could we have ever imagined that our stars wouldn't align that way?

Violet had always seemed to belong to herself. We'd all be having dinner or playing cards, and Violet would be explaining ideas that came from everywhere and nowhere. Fantastic lands that never existed, places where women ruled over men, laughing at the silliness of her father's stern advice on how to approach the world. Her parents would look at each other, bewildered that this creature had come from them, when it was so obvious that she couldn't possibly have come from anywhere. She truly seemed to have just sprung to life out of thin air and she carried a charge that very nearly electrified the air around her. It was times like these, when amidst her parent's utter confusion, she would stare across the table and give a crooked half smile that went all the way to her eyes. A real smile. Happy to challenge everyone in her path. I like to think the smile was meant for me, that she was sharing her chaos with me, but in my heart I know the smile was only for herself.

During their visit today, Mrs. David had asked if I felt like a visit from someone else. I told them I didn't much care who visited me. I mean, if someone is cuckoo enough to come to the nuthouse here and spend time with me, who am I to say 'boo'? Mr. David did something very strange then. He turned to me, and he grabbed my hand and squeezed it. He squeezed it hard and I thought for a minute he was trying hard not to cry. I get so mixed up lately, though, I could have been mistaken. He looked deep in my eyes, and he asked if it would be all right if Luke came and saw me. And then I threw my head back and laughed.

You see, Luke St.John was Violet's boyfriend. If you could say she had one at all. She didn't have time for being tied down yet, she'd tell me, in a voice that sounded very decisive. But, she'd continue on to say that if there was one boy who could keep up with her, it was Luke. They had some kind of understanding, and as far as I knew it was an unspoken one. They seemed to just lock eyes and know what the other was thinking. He never tried to change her though, so to me, he seemed like a pretty stand-up guy. Handsome, in a careless sort of way. Wavy brown hair, an olive complexion and eyes as green as the lake after a gale. He was strong and sturdy, and he had a lightning wit, which is what I think she liked most. I had heard that after what happened he had dropped out of University of Chicago for the semester.

I haven't seen him since, and I haven't expected to. I'm certainly not going to sit and cry with him, if that's what he is looking for. My grief is my own and I'm not going to have a regular blues rag with him. I like Luke, but what is the point of us two kids getting together when the person we both actually want to see, isn't around?

Mr. and Mrs. David seemed confused, and perhaps a little hurt by my reaction. And then I realized that they were being awful sweet to shack me up here. My own folks would probably just have locked me up in a room until I started acting normal again, and who knew when that would be? So, reluctantly, I agreed. Truth be told, I was a little ashamed to be seen here. It was proof positive that no matter what, I wouldn't and couldn't ever be as strong as Violet.

For a second I imagined that they looked slightly deflated that I had come out of my defiance and into subservience. But again, my mind must be playing tricks on me, because by the time I blinked again, they were calling me a "brave girl" and kissing me sweetly on the forehead. They stood up to leave, and Mrs. David cleared her throat, giving the moment a feeling of importance. She looked down at me, smiled sadly and said Luke would be up Thursday next.

As they walked out, I racked my brains trying to remember the last time Violet had seen him, and what she had told me about it.

Doctor's Observation Notes

January 20, 1935

Today patient received a visit from Mr. and Mrs. David. Patient seemed agitated and vacillated between expressions of melancholia and extreme giddiness. When the visitors informed patient of the possibility of another visitor soon to arrive in town, patient exhibited a reaction that would most accurately be described as hysterical. Patient continues to deny reality of her mindset and of the events of last October. Parents of the patient have refused electroconvulsive therapy. Patient will undergo another round of hydrotherapy this week, and if there is no improvement, it is the position of this hospital that the guardians of the patient should be again counseled on the different options for shock therapy.

Emmett Blanchard, M.D.

Transcript of a telephone conversation between Maxwell David and Luke St.John

January 21, 1935

Luke St.John: Hello?

Maxwell David:Hello, Luke? Maxwell David here. Listen, Luke, she's agreed. You can come.

LS: That's great news, sir! What did she say? How is she doing?

MD: Luke, slow down. She's still not herself. She thought it was strange that you wanted to see her at all, but she agreed. We're not sure this is a good idea, but we're not sure it's a bad one. You're expected Thursday.

LS: I see, sir. I understand. Thank you for ringing me, sir. I'll drive up this week.

MD: Safe travels, and as always, our home is your home while you're here.

LS: Thank you, sir. For everything.

Journal

January 21, 1935

One of those days I suppose. Although it seems more and more while I am here that everyday becomes one of "those days". I don't exactly know what they want from me here. I mean, I'm sad. I'm heartbroken. My best friend in the whole world is gone. And all anyone seems to remember about her is that some monster beat the life out of her and then raped her. The more I talk about it, the more I bring her up, the more it seems like they shake their heads in disapproval. I can't just wake up and be cured tomorrow, I wouldn't even know how to pretend. So, I'm at an impasse. I float between wanting to be cured, whatever that may mean, and trying to defend my grief. Grief is allowed. Or at least it should be. Violet would tell me to *feel* any goddam way I please. But, Violet's gone, and I'm all that's left. Who can I look to now?

If they give me another one of these "treatments" I'm either going to drown or die of hypothermia. They call it "hydrotherapy" but I'm not sure how taking a cold bath for hours in the winter is considered therapeutic.

One of the nurses saw me writing the other day, teeth chattering after one of the baths. She knows my story. Everyone here does. I like this nurse, she's young and smiles at me in a real way, you can always tell a real smile from a fake one--it's in the eyes. Her smiles feel encouraging and kind, and a smile from her has come to mean a lot to me. As I was writing she came behind me, but not in a read-over-your-shoulder kind of way, boy I hate that. She just came close and speaking quietly said, "Why don't you write about her? Tell the stories you want people to know? It might help bring her back to you". Which is what I had meant to be doing the whole time, but that cold water must have mixed me up because I had clean forgot that whomever reads this chicken scratch won't have a clue about Violet. So, I thought hard. It's difficult to capture a personality, a life, in a story. But, I aim to do better.

There was this time in Mr. Aaron's science class, where Violet showed her true talent for capturing others. We were about 14 at the time, and Mr. Aaron was lecturing on and on, as he was wont to do. Each sentence drier than the last, our eyes flitted constantly to the immovable clock. I realized that lecture had only started ten minutes prior, and my frustration was echoed by several sighs and yawns around the room. Violet, however, had her science textbook pulled close to her chest, and she sat Indian style and seemed to the whole world to be in her own little wigwam sanctuary. This comfort and happiness must have struck Mr. Aaron as strange, as he was used to apathy and suffering from his students. Violet didn't even look up as he meandered over to her desk and pulled the novel out from inside the book, where she had cleverly stashed it in order to attempt to make the time go by in his class.

With a loud "harrumph!" Mr. Aaron loudly asked her what was more important than his lesson. She looked up at him with a catlike smile. One would almost have thought she had planned the whole thing. Mr. Aaron, mistaking her reaction for embarrassment, asked her if she would like to share with the class, she popped up, smoothed her skirt, shook her hair, and told him, "I'd be delighted, I thought you'd never ask".

She stepped up onto the seat of her desk, and taking her book in hand, she filled us all in on what had happened already, and began to read from the page she had left off on. But what a reading! Her eyes lit up with excitement as she read, impossible romance, daring sword fights, revenge, loyalty. The story came alive under her narration. Even Mr. Aaron looked on, hanging on her entire story. She knew exactly how the voices should sound and her voice came to a crescendo in times of great excitement or violence in the book. When suddenly, she sat down.

Mr. Aaron snapped out of his reverie and asked her to continue. She replied that class had ended five minutes before. Our eyes darted to the clock, and we realized she was right. Slowly, students started to collect their things and move out of the classroom. Violet and I were the last to leave. As we walked by Mr. Aaron's desk, he quietly said that if she would like to finish reading it aloud to the class, he would be amenable to altering the schedule of lessons to accommodate. She offered him the same feline smile, and then winking brazenly, tossed the book she had been reading out of onto his desk. And I am sure we were both shocked to find it was a copy of Emily Dickinson poems.

She had made the whole thing up on the spot, and pretended to read it.

That's just the way she was. She delighted, enthralled and shocked everyone she met. And they loved her for it.

Maybe you begin to understand why she is someone worth remembering. Someone I just can't forget.

Diary of Luke St. John

January 22, 1935

I can hardly confess to myself how often I spend replaying the last time Violet and I were together. That last day. Before it happened, before she was taken away from me. It seems that the girl I'm to go visit is a shade compared to her. A mere shadow of the irrepressible sunlight that was Violet David. But, there are similarities too, and at any rate...maybe there is a connection to be made.

Violet just wasn't like other girls. She wasn't really like anyone. It wasn't only that she was a choice bit of calico, her looks were top shelf. But she sort of seemed to inhabit her own world, and if you were in it, boy, you sure didn't want to be out.

She had a way of making you feel like there was no one on Earth she'd rather be talking to. Like I was the most important person alive, and then at the same time, there was a selfishness. A feeling that really she was the most important person alive. I just happened to be sharing the glow with her. But that was fine by me. A lot of guys think that a girl's a real tot if she's into letting them pet skirt, but that just wasn't on the table for us. She wasn't only a piece for me, she was the

kind of girl you felt lucky just to be around.
And the crazy thing was, she seemed to feel
the same way about me. Tons of guys were
hot for her, but she just laughed at them and
put her arm around me. And it's been like that
since we first met on Michigan Ave. when she
was 12. Inseparable ever since.

That last day though. It didn't feel
special. In retrospect, I don't know why it
would. There was nothing significant. Just a
little necking, some sweet words, mostly from
me-as usual, and then she explained to me this
idea she had. She always had these nutty
ideas that were just gorgeous. They usually
had to do with her being fabulous and
important and sophisticated and she included
me in it as her sidekick. This last night was a
plan. A plan she had for our future. She said
we should move to Paris, and she could model
for Coco Chanel, or help her think of some new
designs. We would live above a Bistro and just
walk downstairs to grab some cafe au lait and
a croissant every morning. When I asked her
what I would do while she was gone working
with Coco, she said that I would be finishing
up my paintings and then she laughed in the
most beguiling way and called me a 'silly
goose'. She was forever calling me that. It
used to irritate me, but it's one of those things,
now that I never hear it, I miss it more than I
thought possible.

When I inquired what paintings I would be finishing, she smiled, that cat-like smile she had, and said she of course would be posing nude for me so that I could become a famous painter. When I smiled back, she slapped me lightly and I told her I had no problem at all with this plan, except... I didn't know how to paint. She snapped back that it was because I'd never seen anything worth painting. And then she winked at me, and kissed me full on the mouth. One of those hard, fast kisses that leaves you needing air, and feeling a little bewildered.

Our whole conversation was taking place in our usual spot, Lou Mitchell's on Jackson Blvd. I'd sneak away from my classes and she'd meet me, and together we'd hole up there, drinking coffee in the middle of the day, or later in the evening, feeling very liberated and grown up. The place was nothing special, except that it was our place. We came here a few times a week, and neither of us told our families, or our friends or anyone where we were going. Sort of an unspoken agreement. When we were at Lou's, we were in our own world... or perhaps I should say we were in Violet's world. And that world was made from beautiful ideas and dreams built by the imagination of this incredible young woman that I had been in love with since the day I laid eyes on her.

Reflecting back now it seems idiotic that we'd keep our whereabouts a secret. I was and am, a damn fool. I was selfish. I wanted her all to myself, even if it was just at Lou's. I blame myself for what happened. If we hadn't made it such a habit, if I had walked her home, it never would have happened. But, I'm getting ahead of myself.

Violet was just mad to move out of the United States. Not because she didn't care for the old stars and stripes, but I think she thought it would make her mysterious to just disappear to France or Belgium or Austria for a while. When I'd remind her that I had a few years left of study at the University, and that when I finished I could find a job abroad, she just huffed and sighed and would pronounce me a "terrible bore". She wasn't the most patient girl in the world, but I think that's another one of the things I liked about her. She thought big, and she thought now.

As she broke away from the kiss. She looked down at her watch and told me she only had another ten minutes, and then she'd have to leave. Her eyes had darted to the corner of the restaurant a few times since we'd been in, and I finally asked her what had so grabbed her attention.

*She turned her face full onto mine,
hunched over, and whispered that there was a
strange man in the back who kept looking at
her. And just as quickly as she had grown
serious, she grew merry again. And continued
telling me all about her plan for our life
abroad. After I had assured her multiple times
that she was indeed beautiful and shapely
enough to model in Paris, and that I would be
in ecstatic fits to paint her, she pressed her
rosy red lips together, gave me another
immobilizing kiss, and stood up quickly. I
remember that I invited her for dinner at my
parent's place for that weekend, and we
agreed to see Miriam Hopkins in "The Richest
Girl in the World" at the Gateway Theatre.*

*And she left. She skipped out the door. I
was in such a haze of paying our check,
thinking about the talkie we'd be going to see,
and picturing me painting Violet in Paris, that
I didn't even watch her walk away. I didn't
even notice if anyone else left around the same
time she did. I didn't notice anything, except
that I was drunk on Violet David once again,
never imagining it'd be the last time I'd see
that cat-like smile, hear the sweetness of her
voice or feel the heat of her lips.*

I was a damned fool.

Journal

January 24, 1935

Curious. I can hardly account for today's events, nor begin to understand them. But, since I am expected to use this journal, I might as well record what happened...and then perhaps something will make sense when I am writing or re-reading it later.

Luke St.John came to visit me today. He came precisely at the time Mr. and Mrs. David told me to expect him. I had forgotten how handsome he was, and for a moment felt a selfish pang of jealousy that he wasn't really there to visit me. I think he saw something of this feeling on my face, because his eyes became very wide, and he reached to take my hand, but the quick movement towards me frightened me, and I found myself shrinking back.

This entire series of actions took no more than ten seconds, but the silence afterward felt like an eternity. I never knew what people meant when they said things like that, "the silence felt like forever" or "in that moment it felt like forever was passing", but I know now. It's a consuming awkwardness of words not said and feelings not expressed.

I sat there, suddenly feeling ashamed of being in an asylum. Of him seeing me here. Of both of us knowing that this sort of thing would never have happened to Violet. He carefully, slowly, took hold of the cold metal chair that sat near the door, and he pulled it so that it was facing me, and about three feet away from where I was sitting. He sat down uneasily and, rested his elbows on his knees, and buried his face in his hands. Again, it was silent in the room.

After a few moments, he dropped his hands and looked into my face, as if he was trying to recognize me. He asked if I remembered him. "of course, I remember you, silly. You're Violet's boyfriend, Luke. How could I forget a thing like that? I'm depressed, not crazy." I said the last part more as a confirmation to myself than to him.

He nodded at me, and slowly one of those unconvinced, upside down smiles that is not exactly a frown, took over his features. He asked me something like, how well did we know each other? And, I gaped at him, confused. He was kidding, right? I mean, I didn't know him as well as Violet, but she had told me plenty. Just what was he driving at? I replied that I imagined we knew each other well enough to have a regular conversation, tilting my head on the last word to indicate that he'd better catch my meaning, and stop all these strange questions.

For a moment, he replaced his head in his hands, and I was worried that he was crying. I realized that even if he wasn't depressed enough to be put away in an asylum, that he was still overwhelmed enough to have taken a semester away from school, and that when all was said and done, they had loved each other very much.

I stood up, and made my way over to him. Kneeling in front of his chair, I grasped his left hand with both of mine, and pulled it down towards me. We looked into each other's eyes, and I think we both saw the same living, spasm of pain that inhabits both of us. For a moment he looked pained, and startled, and I gathered up my courage and said, "We both have lost someone very dear to us. Neither one of us knows how to talk to each other exactly, because the person who brought us together is gone. When Violet's parents first asked if you could come to see me, I didn't understand why, but now I think I do. Because no one else understands. Luke, please come see me again. I don't know why, but when you're here it hurts and it's strange, but it's almost like I can handle it better."

I didn't know then, and I don't know now where those words came from. I really didn't even know that I felt that way until the words were uttered aloud. But as soon as I said them, I knew it was true. There was something familiar, something comforting and loving in his presence, and although in some ways I felt disloyal to Violet by wanting to spend time around Luke, at the same time I had a sense that it didn't matter. She was gone, and we were here. We'd have to find any way we could to get through this. It was like coming up for air in the middle of drowning, he was that first breath of life that confirmed for me that I *could* survive this.

After I was done with my speech, I got back up and sat in my chair, and looked back at him expectantly. His face looked harder, somehow, as if he had made a decision. As if he had assumed a mask to wear until he didn't need it anymore. He thanked me, and then said something strange. He said, "I'll be happy to continue to visit you, and maybe between the two of us we can bring Violet back... even if it's just a little bit". I added, "or put her to rest", to which a grimace of pain broke the mask he had assumed, but it flashed quickly, and it left me altogether undecided if he had looked pained or not.

We spent the next few hours playing a card game, and discussing the talkies, my need for a radio in my room, and he told me some gossip about people we both knew. It was all very safe, no more treading on shaky ground, until he made to leave, that is. He informed me that he would be back to visit in a week or so, and that because he had taken the semester off, he had applied for a part time job at the bank in Traverse City and would be staying with the David's. He wasn't due to start the job until late February, but he would be coming up to visit me again and get himself set up in the meantime.

This all surprised me very much, but his farewell surprised me most of all. As he was walking out the door, he turned around quickly and grabbed me around my shoulders into a hug. I'd never been that close to Luke before, but it felt nice, albeit a little inappropriate. I felt my body stiffen, and then surrender to his embrace. I hadn't been hugged in a long time. He raised his mouth to my ear and whispered, "think of her for me, please. Violet. Think of Violet". As he softly removed himself from the embrace, I looked at him and said, "I always think of her. That's all I think of. That's why I'm here!" and I slammed the door to my cell on his confused face.

I still don't know why I was that angry. What right did he have to hold me like that? What right did he have to come visit me and pay attention to me like that, and all the while to be thinking of Violet? I miss her and love her too, but I can't pretend to be her. Any fool can see that I'm just plain old me. We might have looked alike, we might have been thick as thieves, but I'll never be her. That's my tragedy. But, I'm not made of stone either. It's not fair of him to presume on my feelings. I'm broken too.

So, now I look forward to seeing Luke again, but I also dread it. But, it's better than just feeling empty and alone.

Doctor's Observation Notes

January 24, 1935

Patient received a visitor this afternoon that caused a large degree of agitation. Patient seemed distant and brooding. During our conversation after the visitor left, the patient seemed unsure about where she was, or whom she was speaking with. Her answers to questions about her feelings and state of mind were vague and she looked as if she was preoccupied with other thoughts throughout the examination.

After speaking to the patient's parents, it is the decision of the family that these new developments in her personality may be positive developments. That perhaps she is in some ways coming out of the self inflicted psychosis that she has been suffering from since her breakdown in the autumn of last year. The next time the gentleman comes to visit, the family has asked that the patient be at liberty to walk the grounds of the hospital to allow greater independence of conversation and feeling, while also allowing a staff member to more easily observe their interactions unnoticed by the patient.

Although not our most serious case, it is a puzzling and interesting study nonetheless.

Despite the feelings of my colleagues, I am still hopeful of a full recovery over time. I must admit, however, the challenges that the recovery itself will awake.

Emmett Blanchard, M.D.

Journal

January 26, 1935

My goodness, but it's positively frigid up here. I had always thought Chicago winters were interminable, but I can hardly bear the chilling winds. Which, oddly enough got me to thinking about Violet.

Sometimes, when it's clear, I can look out my window and see all the way out to Lake Michigan. The same waters that touch here could have touched in Chicago, and with that thought in mind, I couldn't help but wonder if some of that freezing cold water could have been the same water we'd spent time splashing around in.

To think less than a year ago we had skipped school and found ourselves fleeing to the 31st street beach. Thanks to the World's Fair of 1933, Chicago seemed like the place to be- it felt like the only place to be. The whole world had wanted to be in Chicago, and here we were two girls splashing away in the waters outside of a great city. Fortunately, through smart financial decisions our families and Luke's had been relatively untouched by the Depression, and because we were younger, (My God, but it seems years and years ago!) and selfish, we just considered ourselves Queens of

Chicago, Queens of the world. I know that Violet had thought about inviting Luke, but in the end decided she didn't want to share her freedom. We just floated around, enjoying the breeze, convincing ourselves it wasn't too cold to be in the water, which it most certainly was.

Such a carefree day. It's unimaginable to me that we could go from there to here. Free as a bird, to as caught as a mouse in a trap. The same water that lapped over our skin, that wetted our hair and got in our eyes... that same water is sitting still, frozen in movement. I know it isn't all frozen, but I guess I'm glad the bit I can see is. At least we have that in common. We both are immutable. Holding our secrets, our memories of free windy days, where we were both kissed by the sun. When spring comes back again will I break out from this prison of myself? This prison of sadness? Will I be like the water and flow freely again? I'm ashamed to say that the thought terrifies me. What does it even mean to be normal again? To be myself? I can't even remember myself. I only remember Violet, and there's no way for her to be reborn with the spring. She's gone. So, maybe I'll just remain this *thing* that I've become, living but not alive. Breathing in, but not feeling that the breath is sustaining me. Like a drowning woman who comes up for air, to be pulled back under the weight of the deep blue.

Today it is Saturday, a day that used to be a welcome respite from the busy-ness of the week. It was a day to do what I chose, to spend reading a book, with Violet, dreaming about the future. Now it's just Saturday. A day of the week, another notch of time. So my life has become a succession of lazy nothings, ice baths and far too many examinations, observations and consultations.

I can barely remember my parents. They don't write. I know they communicate with the doctors here, but not with me. The only visitors I have are the David's and now Luke. Three people who would trade me for Violet in a heartbeat, and seem to resent that I'm here. I survived, and she didn't. They thought she could make it through anything and they feel betrayed that their beautiful, brash, bold girl is dead. And now they are left with a meek, milky, morose substitute. I can't help but feel sorry for them myself. In fact, I'd love to have traded places, because I realize more every day how worthless I am without her.

Journal

February 2, 1935

A lot can happen in a week. I suppose after my last entry I had a bit of a relapse of my melancholia. I had my first round of shock therapy on Sunday. I never thought my parents would authorize that. The David's came up to visit on Monday and were absolutely enraged. Mrs. David came back in muttering about "the hospital betraying their confidence...making decisions in the interest of the patient..medical professionals my foot!"

I told her I was sure that my parents had given it the A-ok. Very tartly, she turned to me and spat her next words at me. "Oh you think so, do you? Well, where are your parents if they care so much about you!?" To which Mr.David, catching her by the arm, quietly asked her to leave the room. After a wave of emotion passed over her face, she quietly did as he had asked.

I didn't remember much of what had happened, some flashes of pain. I felt groggy and tired, and honestly not up to having visitors. In fact, after they left, and all the rest of this week I have spent a lot of time sleeping, or thinking... and when I say 'thinking', I mean, sitting silently and then looking at the clock and realizing I've been in the same attitude for most of the day.

I didn't feel sad this week, I didn't think of Violet very much, but that was mostly because I felt like I couldn't think of anything. Just blank.

Until, yesterday. When it happened.

I had been pulled from my room in the morning by a nurse and an orderly and taken to the treatment rooms for my "hydrotherapy", which again, is a freezing bath for hours at a time. Whoever developed this treatment as a means of curing depression must not have understood the torture the human body undergoes when submerged in icy water.

When I was returned to my room later in the day, I felt faint, but alert. Do not mistake my suffering body for a damaged mind. Depressed I may be, but the wreckage of my body contributed to a heightened sense in the rest of my faculties. It was strange, terrifying, wonderful, horrible to encounter what was so unmistakably *Violet's scent*.Violet was one of those people that beautiful scents just lingered on.

Two people might wear a drop of cologne, or perfume, and on one the scent flares vibrantly and then slowly dies off in a small space of time. While on the other, the scent becomes part of their own. To the point that their scent follows them everywhere they go. Not in a disagreeable, overpowering way, rather the scent mixes with their own pheromones and becomes a part of them. So that, upon entering a room one knows with some certainty that this person has left it not too long ago, because their scent lingers.

This is what had happened to me. I had walked into my room, to find that Violet had most definitely been in that room at some point. It was not a perfume smell, nor any type of artificial scent, it was her natural smell, something I had become accustomed to and familiar with in the course of our close friendship.

But, how? My mind raced over the possibilities, the horror of it being a visitation from her ghost, to the hope that her spirit had deigned to visit me for a benevolent purpose. It also came to my mind that perhaps...it wasn't her ghost at all. Maybe, Violet was not dead. Once this idea came into my mind, I could not dismiss it. It *felt* right. Her smell was so real, almost tangible, it was as if she had just visited and then taken her leave and her scent still lingered after she had made her goodbyes.

If she was, indeed, alive, why did she not announce herself? Why would she hide herself from her family and from Luke? Was she ashamed by what had happened to her? Or did she have a darker design? So many thoughts whirled through my mind, and each new idea brought with it more questions than answers.

I resolved to discuss it with Violet's family and most importantly with Luke. I also realized that perhaps this was the key to unlocking my depression and my path out of this asylum. It was then that I also understood for the first time that I truly did not want to be here. I had thought that it did not matter to me where I was, because Violet was nowhere. But, I saw in that moment that there was an animal part of me that was trapped. An animal that was caged and hungry and fighting to come out of this prison that I was in physically, but also the one that I had created mentally to protect myself from the raw, emptiness of Violet. I understood that I was being consumed by routine, by treatments, and that at some point I would no longer be able to fight.

Either I willed myself to see this through, or I would entrap myself in this attitude. This half-life. Leave it to Violet, alive, dead, or visiting spirit to stir things up. She always found a way to add drama to any situation. To jazz things up, stir the pot, make people sit up and take notice. And I was up; awake finally to the possibility that my melancholia was founded on mist, or...that I was crazier than anyone had imagined.

Confession of Herman Billings,

As recorded by Sgt. Christopher O'Noulain,

November 4, 1934

I had been watching her for a while. The kids would have called her a canary, and she sure was a good looking dame. She met that young fella at Lou's a couple times a week, and after I followed them around a little and got to know their routine. People sure can be ignorant. They don't notice you at all if you look ordinary. She never seemed to notice me at all. I liked it better that way. I knew I had picked the perfect girl to teach a lesson to.

She was kissin' all over that fella, and then she headed for the door. He didn't even see me follow her out. We got a few blocks away, and I was walking no more than two arm lengths behind her. That stupid bird didn't even know I was there. So, real smooth-like, when we came up to a quieter part of town, I pushed her into the alley and laid a couple of good punches at her face. She clawed back pretty good. I made sure not to hit her in the mouth, the mouth always bleeds a lot and teeth come out...it's a mess. I went for the sides of her head, hoping to knock her out. It's so much easier when they can't fight ya. Some

*guys like it when they struggle, but not me. I
like to just teach 'em a lesson and have my
way and then leave. Real easy like. She was
an angry cat though. Spitting and clawing,
kicking and biting. Hollering like all get out.
That won't do. That won't do at all. I laid a
few sharp kicks right to her abdomen, heard
some ribs snap and then hit her head into the
alley wall. She was done fighting for a while.
So, I went to work. It's always easy when
they're wearing a dress. A couple seconds into
it though, she started moaning real funny,
and at first I thought she might be enjoying it.
But then the blood started coming out of her
mouth and I realized I needed to get out of
there. I wasn't about to make good with a
corpse.*

*If she was about to kick it though, I
needed to be sure she was really gone. I gave
her a few more kicks to the stomach, a few in
the head and then I slowly walked out of the
alley. Luckily, I didn't have a drop of blood on
me. I realized I had a few strands of her hair
on my shoe, and I casually picked them off
and dropped them in the street.*

*I was far from satisfied. I had an eye on
that little bitch for weeks. I had spent a lot of
time planning out how that would go down. I
knew she'd be a fighter, but I figured when she
realized she'd met her match she'd see that
she'd just need to lay there and bow to the*

wishes of her new master. She was always bossin' that young kid around and wrappin' him around her finger, I know what girls like that want. They want a lesson. I was the one to teach it to her. But, apparently she doesn't like to learn. I guess she wasn't as strong as I'd figured she'd be. It's a shame. I expected better. I've done lots of girls before, and the dumber they are the easier they are to pluck. Guess these smart girls aren't so smart after all. Can't be smart if you're getting your head rammed into a wall.

So, yeah. I did it. I followed her. I swatted her around. I had "been" with her. I left her there to die. And I'd do it again.

Journal

February 6, 1935

The weather seems to have shifted slightly, as it felt a bit warmer today. As a result, before my visitors came early this morning, I obtained permission from Dr. Blanchard to take a stroll outside with the nurse I've gotten to like. We don't talk much, but she seems to have a silent sympathy for me, and a quiet smile that looks as if it hides more than it reveals. She isn't a friend, but she is kind, and kindness in a place like this is not to be taken for granted.

The air was bracing, but it was good. It was a healing cold, not like the cold of the baths I had been subjected to. It made me feel powerful to choose to be out in that cold. It wasn't unbearable, and I was bundled up like an Inuit, but it still was a kind of freedom to be moving about the world, albeit a very small space of world, and to be facing it on my own terms. To be choosing my own steps rather than following the directions or the lead of a nurse, doctor, orderly. I felt myself smile. And it felt on my face like the same feline smile that Violet would have given. A smile that represents a woman who is coming into her own, and approves of herself. Yes, the walk was doing me worlds of good.

We wandered around the buildings for another quarter of an hour. I began to see plainly what type of place I was in. It is surprising how much different a place can come to look in one's mind when one only sees the inside of it. The mind has a way of imagining the exterior of a place based on the experience of the interior. And I'm sure it works the other way around also. However, I found that my imaginings bared little resemblance to the structures before me. There are many buildings that make up the hospital, and I think it likely that the patients are kept in different buildings according to gender and severity of case. I found myself wondering what level of sanity I possessed and where I fell in the totem of mental disease here.

The hospital is built of brick, and there is a disconcerting amount of metal cage-like meshing over the porches and windows. Through the mesh I could see the vacant eyes of other people, some seemed to watch me, which I must confess sent shivers down my spine for some reason, and others simply seemed to follow my movement with their heads. But in a way that suggested they would have done the same had I been a rolling tumbleweed or a squirrel. They saw the movement, yet saw nothing. To me this type of loss, this complete loss of cognizance, loss of self, was demoralizing and a reminder of the possibility of my own loss. To have forgotten one's self seems to be the greatest loss of them all, worse even than death.

The asylum, it's purpose notwithstanding, is a handsome structure in an of itself. The walls give it an air of strength and it is not without attractions and design, but I think it is enough that in generations to come those who find themselves among these buildings, or perhaps even farther on than that, when the bricks themselves have crumbled down to rubble, those that find themselves walking in this place will feel an eerie emptiness. A theft of their happiness, even for but a moment. A whisper of sorrow will sweep over them and leave their hearts a bit heavier than before they were in this place. There is too much disappointment here. Too much confusion and pain, too much loss, and not enough finding. I would dare to say that too few of the lost here, ever find their way back to happiness or sanity. But, it occurred to me that in these thoughts I was treating myself as somehow not belonging to this place, and remembering that I was one of the lost, I silently vowed to trek my way out. To find whatever was left of Violet, and escape.

The nurse reminded me that I would be expecting visitors soon, and that I should ready myself for their arrival. I breathed in one final, independent breath, and submitted myself to be herded back indoors. I did have quite a bit that I wanted to discuss with my visitors today, and with that thought in mind, I quickened my step in order to bring myself to a conversation that would at least ruffle some feathers, if not offer me answers.

Around 11:00am, Mr. and Mrs. David arrived. I watched them walk up to the door of my building, and I watched as they looked at one another and then Mr. David squeezed his wife's hand, and I read his lips when he said, "it'll be all right, Alice". Then giving her hand another squeeze they stepped into the asylum. It occurred to me then, how strange it was that they continued to visit me. I had been Violet's friend, but what was I to them? I began thinking, perhaps Violet *was* alive, and the David's knew it! They knew it and they visited me here thinking I knew where she was and that if they were kind to me, I'd reveal it. Or maybe they were keeping me here as bait to lure Violet. I dismissed both of these ideas almost as soon as they came into my mind. But there *had* to be a reason that they visited me, paid for my expenses here, a reason that they had taken me off my parent's hands when I had my breakdown and brought me here in the first place. I saw that this was another piece of the mystery that I would have to fit into place.

When they walked into the room, I was taken aback by how thin Mrs. David looked. Mr. David appeared to have aged ten years, and I couldn't help but wonder if I had even noticed these changes before, or if they were more recent. Had they looked like this since the situation with Violet, and I had just been too wrapped up in myself to notice? I shuddered to think of how far gone I had been. We made small talk for some minutes. They observed that my complexion looked healthier, and that the doctors had said I had gained some strength. They looked very pleased, and I was glad that my progress could offer them some degree of happiness. I asked after their own health, and Mr. David softly patted his wife's arm, and his eyes seemed to appraise and take in her fragility, her sadness, and with no little affection, he replied "day by day, my girl. We take it, day by day."

I had thought to ask after my parents, but I was alarmed to discover that it had been so long since I had seen them, that I was unable to remember much of anything about them. I also felt a sort of release, because although I knew this should bother me more, I saw immediately that it did not bother me all that much. And so, for some odd reason, I felt more relaxed, as if I didn't need to worry about them. Additionally, I added to myself, I had enough to worry about right then.

So instead, I asked after Luke. I was sure that he was supposed to be visiting with them today, and so when Mrs. David looked stricken by my question, I found my face growing hot. I thought perhaps I had made an error, maybe the David's thought that I was asking because I did not prefer their company, or perhaps they were offended by the idea that I might have developed a crush on their beloved daughter's beau. But, no. None of these was the cause for alarm. Mr. David leaned in, away from Mrs. David and told me in a calming quiet voice that Luke would be back in a few days. He apologized for his wife and said that my question had merely surprised her, and that she was easily excitable lately. She didn't want to bring me any disappointing news in the asylum, and she had been afraid that the news would upset me.

It seemed that Luke had been devastated by our last meeting, and so needed a few more days before he could endure another visit. Mrs. David now leaned forward and assured me, as if I was a small child or an injured bird, that it wasn't that Luke didn't want to see me, God forbid, but instead that the whole ordeal had been extremely traumatizing for him too, and he didn't want to bring more stress to me by coming. This all left me feeling very confused. It was in some ways, flattering, but also a little obnoxious. I tried to think of what Violet would do in a similar situation. Violet would have laughed at them both outright and told them to stop being such old ladies. She would have languidly reclined in her chair, crossed her legs and put her index finger to her lips. She then would have taken that finger and wagged it at them as if they were silly children and then she would have swooped down and grabbed both of their hands, squeezed them and enthusiastically declared both of her parents to be, "little dears!" And so, I did all of these things. I don't know why. It was almost as if Violet's spirit had taken over my body and I was going through these motions against my will.

The reaction was not what I expected. Mrs. David almost seemed to swoon, and Mr. David looked at me with an expression of hopeful confusion. He squeezed my hand back, and gave me a confidential look, and said, "let's talk in a moment. Let me take Mrs. David back to the car to rest." Mrs. David gave me a weak smile, nodded her head a few times and then allowed herself to be escorted out. After they left the room, I sat upright in my chair and looked down at my hands, wondering what had possessed them. Wondering what had come over me? And all the while, feeling no closer to finding the answers I needed.

I peered out the window, watching Mrs. David clutch closer to her husband as he led her out to the car. It had started snowing, just the light, cottony snow that melts as soon as it hits the ground. I felt the corners of my mouth curve, and felt somehow warmer. It was comforting to know that though the world had been frozen, it would slowly thaw and become spring again. I took it as a metaphor for my present circumstances. And yet, I knew I never would be the same. A part of me was dead. I pondered these things, swaying between feelings of light happiness and a sort of twisted sadness, until Mr. David returned.

He sat across from me, as Luke had done on his visit. He looked me full in the face, and talked to me. Without restraint, or awkwardness. We discussed books, writing in my journal (though not the particulars), the weather, the food, the nurses, the views of the lake. It wasn't deep and penetrating conversation, but I felt *normal*. Or at least like a human being, and less like a zoo animal. I was, in a word, elated. I had spent so much of my time lately during visits in painful, safe, restrained voices, awkward pauses, that I had forgotten what it was like to just be talked to. With the exception of Luke's visit, which had been lovely, but had been marred by his strange behavior, this was the first real conversation I could remember having, since...before.

When our conversation was coming to a close, he reached for my hands, and held them in both of his own. His hands were large, warm and strong. He inspected my face for a moment, and appearing as though he had found something within my expression that he had been looking for, he nodded his head and proclaimed, "Ahh, I have hope for you yet. We'll show them, won't we?" And I eagerly agreed, though I had no idea exactly *what* I was supposed to show to *whom,* but it was one of those moments where agreeing was the only option, and I was happy to do so.

As I watched him leave, I felt a change that day. A change in my relationship with Violet's parents, and a change within myself. Something that I had long forgotten, and still couldn't quite remember. Some secret, some important fact that I needed to know. Instead of it frustrating me that I was unable to remember it, I was glad. Glad in the knowledge that there was something about me that was worth remembering, even if I wasn't sure what it was at the moment.

Diary of Luke St.John

February 6,1935

I have just heard what could be very good news from the David's. They seemed excited and led me to believe that our little patient may be recovering. It is wonderful to see them so full of hope; it is marvelous to see that they can still feel hope about something after all they have endured these past few months. I desperately wish I could share their optimism.

I felt guilty for not visiting with them today. But, truth be told I want my next few visits to be on my own. I want to ascertain for myself just exactly what she knows, what she remembers, what secrets she might not even know she's guarding.

You see, I got to thinking after re-reading my last journal entry about another aspect of this whole thing...that I'm not sure how keen I am to have it brought out unintentionally by a confused young woman. It was on that last day, when Violet had been so jazzed about moving to Paris, it was that conversation that brought out a memory of another time Paris had held meaning for the two of us. (As if I could ever forget!)

Near the end of the summer, August it was, last year. Violet had convinced me to take her, yet again, to the World's Fair. She loved the foreign pavilions, especially the "Paris City Streets". We walked in and saw one of Sally Rand's provocative fan dances. It was erotic, sensual, and exciting. Violet thought so too. I could tell by the squeeze of her hand, and in the fervor when her eyes met mine. Like I'd said before, I'd been in love with Violet for a long time, and although she could be wild and shocking--we weren't in a hurry, if you catch my drift. Not that I never thought about it, I'd be crazy not to. She was a marvel, with her full red lips, long wavy honey hair. She was wearing a jaunty little cap that day, and her eyes seemed clear and I could feel the same urgency in her that I was feeling. Her lips twisted to the side, she swung around so that she was directly in front of me, pressed close to my chest, and she whispered, gently but with an air of conviction, "It's time to go".

I don't remember leaving the fair, or arriving back to her house, I don't even remember walking up the stairs. I had imagined this day so many times, and in my imagination I had been so much more brave, so much more sure of myself. I found that the same needing, wanting, aching feeling that I had was reflected back in her eyes. It briefly crossed my mind that perhaps her parents were at home, and as if reading my thoughts she whispered something about her parents attending the theater. I was nervous, I was excited... I felt alive to all of the possibilities of my youth, my ignorance and my desire.

To my delight, she was the one who seemed confident, and I was more than happy to follow her lead. The room was in half light, the sun making its final exit from the day, the faint fingers of its rays loosing their grip on the room. An old Cole Porter record softly played from some unseen phonograph, the lilting words surrounded us, perfectly describing the moment we found ourselves in, although we would both find later that we did not know the words or what song had been playing at all.

For as much time as we had spent talking, for this one time since the day she'd become "my girl", (as much as any person could say that Violet David was theirs) we were strangely silent. It felt sacred, and exciting and dirty and wrong and wonderful. We undressed, and it wasn't as awkward as I had imagined it would be, and although I'd never seen a naked woman before, (at least not in real life), I have to say that Violet was the most dazzling thing I'd ever seen. We moved together, and I felt her arch her back beneath me, it was all kisses and warm breath and her hair splayed out over the pillow. I knew in that moment that I would never love

*any girl like I loved this one. Come what may,
or whatever the future held, even if she left me
tomorrow, I could admit to myself that I had
given my body and soul to Violet David, and I
was surprised to realize that I had done so a
long time ago. That sharing this moment, this
lovemaking, was only a confirmation of
something I had always known. I'm not sure if
we both found release, as I am not an
experienced lover, nor can I pretend to be still.
But, I think we both felt a wave of change in
our relationship. I think that if she had been
trying to discover anything about me, or the
way I felt, that there is no question all
answers were laid bare. When we declared
ourselves, it seemed to hit somewhere deeper.
I held her to my chest, on her purple satin
sheets, and breathed her in. I knew her smell
as well as I knew the features of her face, and
it's that warm, honeyed scent that fills my
memory now as I write these words.*

*So imagine the trouble I had breathing
when I entered that asylum cell, and that
heady scent filled my nose and lungs. I was
suffocating on her memories. When I had lost
everything about my love, how had her smell
remained? How had her scent lived on in the
company of this sad, confused creature that I
faced in the asylum? It was too much to bear.
The happiness of that moment flooded my
brain, and ravaged my heart and had left me*

broken in that moment, in front of a girl more broken than myself.

How much did she know? Had she revealed any of our secrets to the doctors? Had she told the David's? I am a coward. I am worried for myself, but also, in her confusion and distress, I would not want her to inadvertently reveal any of the secrets that she might have.

I do not even know if it would make it easier or harder to bear for her parents to find out that Violet had given herself to me before the incident. That her maidenhood had been freely given instead of violently stolen. I'm not sure if it matters, since such violence was done in any case. As selfish as it might be, I hold it as a very slight comfort that the love of my life knew physical love that was good, and pure and tender before she had it brutally forced upon her.

Later this week I return to the asylum. I hope that it will do good for both her and myself. I just pray that I do not feel the presence of my beloved as strongly as I did before. It is hard enough to make the visit without it. And at the same time... I must admit it is my most fervent wish to feel the presence of Violet wrap around me once again.

Maybe the best place for us all is an asylum.

Journal

February 9, 1935

I had a visit from Luke today. If possible it was odder than his first, but I'll get to that in a moment. First, I am fairly bursting with a discovery that I made last night.

Since I had first caught her scent in the room after treatments a few days ago, I had thought that a few times I had picked up on it again. My mind went to wild places then, wondering if she was alive and had slipped into my room while I was out. But after last night, I'm not sure what I think anymore.

Just at the moment I imagine that I am firmly grasping hold of my emotions, mastering my sanity, overcoming my sadness, my loss, my confusion, well, I go and find her belongings in my drawer.

It was late last night, I was thinking of my life. Trying to remember what my existence had been like *before*. All of my memories were of her. Were of *us*. Of the stories she'd told me, her pains, her sorrows, her triumphs. I couldn't see where the thread of her life ended and mine began. How could I become so close to a person to lose such sight of myself? How could I have intertwined my life so irrevocably with hers? It was sick. This is the reason that I am here. That I let her in so close, that when she was gone...there was less of me.

I sat there, on the cold metal chair, feeling terribly sorry for myself. Hardly knowing what I was doing, I was opening and closing the drawers of the desk in my room. It was nice to distract myself from the melancholy thoughts that had overtaken me, and the drawers made a delightful grinding creak that filled the room. So I continued, from the bottom drawer and moved up on my very utilitarian vanity, finishing with the middle drawer at the top. I was hardly thinking of what I was doing. I had no object in mind, I fully intended on finding nothing. I pulled the drawer out, and began to slam it closed again, when my attention was grabbed by the contents. A beat up copy of *Wuthering Heights*, which I didn't recognize and tossed aside. But the next thing I drew out was unmistakable. A hairbrush. I'd know it anywhere. For how often she had it out, dragging it through her hair, pulling it through those spun-gold strands. It was embossed and silver plated. I had always thought it was beautiful, something like a Queen would use, much better than the nasty celluloid ones most of the girls our age owned. She'd had it ever since I could remember, and as I reached down to run my finger through it's bristles, a solitary hair was waving out. It had to be hers. The same color, the same shine, the same almost curl. But then again.... I reached for my own undone tresses. My hair was the same. I'd forgotten how alike in looks we were. But, could I have been using her brush all this time and never even noticed it? I glanced around the room, searching, and on my nightstand sat my own green celluloid brush. I walked over to it, clutching the silver plated brush as if it were an infant, to my chest. I picked up my own, turned it over, and compared the hair to the silver brush. They looked the same. It was uncanny. It scared me to think I had a corpse's hair. I wondered briefly if it was true, what they said, that your hair continued to grow after you died.

I shuddered, and I felt a little sad, to think of her long, beautiful hair in that cold grave, growing longer and longer with no one to care for it. I shook my head and laughed at myself. Who cares about her hair? She's DEAD! I silently cursed and admonished myself for my stupid, silly notions. I wandered back to the vanity, reached in, and searched about until my fingers grasped a hold of one more small object. Setting it into the middle of my palm, I saw that it was a locket. I didn't remember her ever having worn a locket, nor have I ever worn one. It wasn't anything special, just a brass, art deco styled pendant on a long chain. I had shrugged my shoulders, and made to replace it in the drawer when, on a whim I opened it. So curious! In one side was a picture of Mrs. David from when she was maybe a year older than Violet and I, perhaps 18 or 19. She looked irrepressibly lovely. The picture looked older and more faded than the one on the opposite side of the locket, which was unmistakably a picture of Luke with a rakish grin on his face. I brought the locket closer to my face, in order to get a better look at it. My, but he is handsome. He must have had the picture done at University and gave it to her as a gift. I wouldn't be surprised if he'd given her the locket too.

I felt it then. A mix of emotions that both frightened and confused me. I was holding on to Violet's things. Her treasures. I was pawing them as if they were mine, looking through them like some crazed voyeur of her personals. I was disgusted with myself, and then I grew even more angry with myself to realize that I was jealous. I was jealous of her beautiful brush and her handsome beau. I wanted them both for my own. I even wished that the locket had been a gift to me from Luke, I could almost imagine him giving it to me. Wrapped up in a box with a purple satin bow. My favorite. Or was purple Violet's favorite? I could hardly remember. I could see his excitement, his desire that I should like it, that I should treasure it, for to treasure the locket with his picture inside was a confirmation to him that he, too, was treasured. I could see myself throwing my arms around him, and kissing his cheeks and hair, positively paralyzed with happiness. Maybe I was remembering him giving it to Violet, maybe she'd told me all about it. I didn't know anymore. And for that moment, I didn't care. I ran the brush through my hair, sticking my tongue out at an invisible Violet. I'd loved her very much, but I was alive and she was dead. I could use her things if I wanted to. I then carefully placed the locket and chain around my neck. Hiding it under my dress, where it came to rest right on top of my heart. It was my secret. Maybe I was lusting after Luke. Maybe I always had. I couldn't remember. It didn't matter, he was still in love with a dead girl. My cold, dead friend. Even if I was betraying her, she had betrayed me too. She left, didn't she? Left me all alone in this solitude of pain.

Oh, dear. I do sound crazy. Perhaps I will have to write about Luke's visit tomorrow morning. I've too much on my mind right now, and I need some time to think through what happened with him here today. In my sadness, (madness?) I've become a monster.

Witness Statement of Irma Coombs, Waitress, Lou Mitchell's

November 4, 1934

I knew both of the kids. They came up to Lou's once a week or so, different days every time. They were real sweet on each other. Always talking and giggling; it was charming. The girl seemed a bit forward for my own taste, especially since she looked to be a few years younger than her beau. She had him twisted up all right. They never caused no trouble, or made too much noise.

I don't remember anything special about that last time they came to eat, it seemed like any of the other times they were in. They sat across the table from one another, slightly hidden from the front door, they were usually holding one of each other's hands across the table. Her hair was always down, and long and a little wild looking. I always noticed her hair because it was striking, and not cut in a fashion that most young ladies kept. She always looked like she was nearly breathless, like she'd run a long distance to be where she was and that she was fairly nervous at having to sit still for any time together. Now the boy, he always looked cool and calm. He appeared to take in everything around him, while never taking his eyes off of her. Like she was hypnotizing him or something. It was remarkable the hold they had on each other. Guess that's how it always seems when you're young, like every moment is the most important one you'll ever have. They both had gone through a couple of cups of coffee, and she had asked, as usual, if she could get four pickles, which she would eat quickly, one after another as if they were a delicacy that one couldn't find at any diner in town.

Now, the only things that stick out in my memory from that day was a fella in one of the back booths who seemed to have his eye on her, or the both of 'em. I thought at first that maybe he was 'a little near' if you catch my meaning, but then he got up and left when she did, and it did seem a little odd...but then again I see odder things almost every day here at the restaurant. The boy seemed a little moonier than usual after she left, and I had been surprised that he hadn't walked her out, but she had seemed like she was in some sort of a hurry.

Then something really funny happened. Another girl walked in to Lou's, and she said something real loud to the boy. I didn't quite catch it, because I was busy with a customer, but she walked right up to him and her face shook with anger or hurt, I couldn't say which. Some strong emotion in any case. He got real defensive, and put his hands up and kept repeating, "not here, not here. For godssakes not here!". I bustled up to the both of them and asked them if there was a problem. The girl twisted her mouth, shook her head, and was wringing her hands. Her chest was heaving in her dress, and I remember thinking that if she got herself any more worked up that those buttons on her dress were bound to pop right off. The boy apologized, and then, grabbing his peacoat, and throwing it over his arm, he twirled a scarf around his neck, and then grabbed her by the crook of her elbow and led her out. The whole time he was talking to her real calm and then I caught him saying, "I told you no more..." and that's all I got before they disappeared out the door.

I can't say rightly that there was anything else that I remember. The girl that came in all angry and huffin' looked a bit like his girl, but had her hair shorter, and waved. She looked a little older too, more his own age. The man who followed the girl out the restaurant, I had never seen him before, or since-- until the officers showed me a picture today when I was brought into the station.

I'm sorry, but I don't remember anything else. A lot of people come into the restaurant, I can't keep an eye on everyone.

Journal

February 10, 1935

Well, I've had a talk with Dr. Blanchard. He has confirmed that no one will be reading my journal if I don't want them to. Which made me feel much more comfortable after all the crazy things I have been recounting and sharing lately in here. (Maybe I *should* be allowing someone else to read these rants)

Luke's visit yesterday. As I wrote before, I had found the hairbrush and the locket the night before he came to see me. It was with the same strange feelings of guilt and perhaps a slight apprehension at seeing him that I readied myself to face him the next morning. Because of Violet's parent's influence over the hospital I am allowed some freedom with my toilette and dress that other patients here are denied. Exercising this freedom for the first time, I decided to take full advantage of my rouge and to take my time in the bath. I wanted him to see me. I wanted him to see me *for me,* and not as the sick, sad girl he had been faced with the last time. I could at least try to make myself presentable. It came to my attention that there was no mirror in my room. Had there ever been? How could I not have noticed that? Doing the best I could without the mirror, I tied my hair into a ribbon and left it lazily waving to the side. I pinched my cheeks, added a little lip rouge, just enough to make myself appear as if I was in a little better health. Perhaps to cause him to wonder whether I'd been taking more exercise than I had been. I wanted to appear, *healthy*. I couldn't stand to have him look at me with pity again. He never pitied Violet, only adored her. And if I couldn't be adored, I at least didn't want his sympathy.

I chose a black jersey dress with a white dove print. The three-quarter sleeves made me feel less restricted in my movements, and the birds gave me a feeling of levity, as if I could fly my way out of the hospital and into happiness again. I finished the last button and was arranging the ruffles on the bodice when I heard the knock on the door. I smoothed my hands down the front of the dress, and realized how fast my heart was beating. And I wondered to myself if all of this preparation and dressing up had been a silly idea. Had I made myself appear more pathetic in the attempt? With hardly any time to change my mind, I cleared my throat and in the clearest voice I could muster, I called out, "Come in".

Luke opened the door and seemed to drink me in like a glass of water. I felt a little anxious, but at last he smiled. He told me I looked like "a real deb", which I remembered was a favorite slang term of his. It made me think of another one of his favorite sayings, which he had said to Violet with some frequency. He'd say, "cash or check?" which was jazz for "shall we kiss now or later?" It always had made Violet giggle and she'd gift him a smooch right then and there. I felt the corner of my mouth lift at the memory, and I raised my eyes to get a good look at him.

It appeared that he had taken some care with his appearance as well. He was wearing two toned oxfords, a crisp white shirt with a grey tie, a grey vest, a grey jacket and grey pants. He had a flat cap on, and was carrying a striped scarf and pea-coat on his arm, as if he had just removed them, but planned on replacing them both soon. He hardly looked real. He was always crisp and clean, his hair styled just-so, as if it had been no effort at all to get dressed and ready and he had simply floated to his destination from wherever he had started. Never ruffled, never a hair out of place...although I noticed now that his face looked worried, anxious and flustered. He had finally broken his cool. Or Violet had. I began to perceive that I had paid little to no attention to his appearance or anyone's for the last few months.

He held out his arm to me, and asked if I had my coat. I had forgotten we were to go walking on the property. He mentioned nonchalantly that the air was milder out today than it had been, and that it would be lovely to take a turn around the grounds. He said it in a way that suggested we were going to be walking around the gardens of a palace rather than the limited area afforded for walking at an asylum in the wilds of Northern Michigan. I walked to my closet and took out my long wool coat, popped a cap over my hair, and he then came closer to help me with my wrappings. When I turned around, we were very close to one another. I thanked him, and as if he had not heard me, it sounded as if he had whispered "beautiful". Thinking I must be imagining things, I tilted my head down to tie the belt on my wrap coat. I noticed that the chain of my locket had begun to protrude out the top of my dress, and in a moment it registered with me that I was not the only one who had noticed it poking out. Quicker than a snake strike, Luke's hand had darted towards the rogue chain and yanked it out. The locket came flying out the top, and before I could say anything or take it away from him, he had it opened and his face filled with hurt bewilderment.

I didn't know what to say. I didn't know what to do. I was at a loss. I felt that I had done something that was monumentally wrong. That I had desecrated a secret trust, or that I had defaced a work of art. His eyes seemed to ask a question, but it was as if they were speaking a different language, because I could make no sense of it and could not even begin to answer. Finally he spoke.

In a sort of lifeless, disembodied voice, with no emotion or feeling, he asked, "Is this some kind of joke? What exactly are you playing at? What is happening?" The tone of his voice was so far from matching the words he was saying that it took me a few moments to register his feelings or his meaning. I looked down at the locket, and back at his face, then back down to the locket and I began sobbing. I snatched the locket out of his hands and shoved it into the top of my dress. I stammered out an explanation of how I'd found it. I omitted the feelings I'd had about seeing his picture, and I also failed to reveal that I had wanted her things to become my own...and instead told him something to the effect that it made me feel close to her.

With bile rising in my throat as I was making these explanations, I saw clearly that it wasn't feeling close to her, or wanting her things... I discerned through all of the lies I had told myself that in actual point of fact, now that she was gone, I didn't want to be like her, I wanted to *be* her.

I let that sit for a moment, both my epiphany and the explanation I had given Luke. He seemed less upset, and was nodding his head for about half a minute. He breathed in and breathed out hard, as if he'd made up his mind about something. Without raising his head, his eyes moved upward to meet mine, and he said, "Why did you keep my picture in the locket?" He said it clearly, and I could tell he had mastered himself completely before asking me. I replied lamely, something about how I believed it belonged there. I could feel myself coloring though, and the heat rushed to my face. One look back at him confirmed that he'd seen through my lie. He considered this for a moment, and then, nodding his head once again, he muttered, "we'll see about that." and then turning to look at me full in the face, he offered his arm and gave me a look that I took to mean, "Shall we?" Interlacing my arm with his, we walked down the hall, down the steps and out into the world.

I hadn't been outside very many times since I had arrived at the asylum. Most of the visits outside were done with my nurse, and I usually just wandered around deep in thought, barely perceiving anything around me. Today though, on his arm, I felt strong and alive and alert. My senses were heightened, the cold was colder, the air was more bracing, the winter smell was fading and I could feel a soft waft of spring. As the wind blew, my hair scattered out around me, dancing in the wind like so many butterflies. I stopped to pick up the ribbon that had been ineffective at keeping it tied to the side. We walked around, companionably for the first few minutes, saying little or nothing.

Luke then looked forward, and spoke. It was more like a pronouncement than a compliment, and I still am not sure what it was meant as. "I like seeing that locket on you. It makes me very glad that it is being worn and cherished again." I thanked him, and assured him that I did indeed cherish it. I longed to put the emphasis on cherish, in order to maybe awkwardly reveal my feelings, but the word 'cherish' in itself stirred a feeling of deep emotion on his face, and so I left my words to remain courteous but platonic. We walked purposefully for a few more minutes, and I allowed myself to feel happy. I allowed myself to pretend that we were walking somewhere beautiful, and that we were what we appeared to be, a young, dapper couple enjoying a walk together. Instead of a mental patient being visited by the beau of her dead bosom friend. I forced all of that from my mind by sheer will, and we continued on, making comments about this or that.

All at once, Luke looked at me, and it appeared that he was about to tell me something, but then his face changed and he blurted, "Oh! But you're freezing! Gosh, I'm sorry doll. I should have been taking better care of you!" Before I could protest and tell him that I was feeling just fine, he was hustling me back to the door and walking me back to my room. As we reached my room, he made a movement as if he was going to leave, and without thinking, I reached out and grabbed his hand. I implored him, rather hysterically, to stay just a little longer. He looked surprised, and coming to face me, took my other hand, and asked if I was sure. Of course I was sure, and gathering a firmer hold on my emotions and speech I called him a goose, (which he certainly was!). He gave me a funny look, but other than that, he looked perfectly natural when he came to sit across from me on the metal chair. All of a sudden, as if an uninvited guest had come to join us, I could smell it. That light, warm Violet smell. It wasn't like a perfume, it was just the smell of *her*. Of course she had come. Of course she was here. Even in spirit she had to have him all to herself. And before I could bite my tongue, I told Luke all of the times I had noticed it. I told him about her scent, and how I would often come back into the room and it would be hanging there like an essence or an aura. As if she'd come for a visit and I'd just missed her. His eyes had been wide at the beginning, but by the time I got to the end of the confession, he was smiling. He admitted that he'd noticed her scent in my room also. He admonished me for feeling crazy, and said that it was perfectly sane to notice pieces of her surrounding me. "After all, you two were very close, correct?" I was surprised by his reaction, but very pleased. I acknowledged that we had been close, and he then did something very strange. He leaned forward, put one finger under my chin and raised my head on level with his own, for a moment my heart caught in my chest; I was sure he was about to kiss me. Instead, with a sly look in his eye, he asked me simply, "Tell me about the day you and Violet met." And all at once I was seized by the opposing desires to talk about Violet, and the repulsion of not wanting to discuss her at all. I had wanted him to kiss me, and his mind, of course, was still on Violet. I replied petulantly that I'd rather not. He insisted, and I prepared to make a snarky comment in return; to my amazement, however, I became conscious of the fact that even if I had wanted to share... I could not for the life of me remember.

How could this be? The confusion on my face seemed to amuse Luke, who sat back into his chair and crossed his arms around his chest. He looked very smug and in that moment I hated him. My mind was locked against me, and struggle how I may, I could not remember a single detail about how we'd met. I'd felt like I'd always known her, I couldn't remember meeting her, but I also couldn't remember ever *not* being around her. I was baffled. I sat back into my chair and fairly drew into myself like a turtle into his shell. I was reminded of being in math class as a child, and wildly flailing my arm to answer the question...only to be called on and find that I did not have an inkling as to what the answer was or how to solve the problem. It was the same surprise at my own ignorance, the same shame in being perceived as a failure. When I looked back up at his face, his eyes had become serious again, and he conceded that he knew things were a bit fuzzy for me right now, and he wasn't trying to upset me. But right on the tail end of that statement, he tacked on, "At least can you tell me a little bit about your family? You must miss them. And I must admit I've never met them." Taking this as a gesture of goodwill that he was interested in *me,* I smiled and started to recount a short biography of my family. But when I tried to begin, my mind became a fuzzy slate. Just hazy figures with no discernible features or faces. Horror coursed through me, and I did my best to push it back down, into the pits of my psyche. How was it possible that I couldn't recall a single thing about my own family? Was it the trauma? Was it being separated from them for so long? And who was "them"? Why couldn't I remember?

I mustered a small smile, and said I didn't want to talk anymore today. At first he seemed hurt, but then a smile flooded his face. "It was awfully nice to see you, doll. Can I come again next week?" I blurted out that he could come again tomorrow, and then instantly regretted the effusive demonstration of my feelings. He didn't seem to have noticed though, and admitted that he would like to, but that he would be busy the next few days, with some loose ends to tie up in Chicago. We both stood up and I walked him to the door. He seemed to be leaving in relatively greater ease than when he had arrived, and I allowed him to lightly brush his lips against my cheek before he tipped his cap, gave me a wink and promised to visit again as soon as he could. He appeared to be relieved, whether it was because he was finally able to leave or if the visit itself had been a salve, I could not be sure.

As the door closed, I turned, ran to my bed and threw the covers over my head. Crying bitterly for the life that I wanted, the one I couldn't remember, and for the knowledge that I didn't know a single thing about myself anymore. The only life I remembered was Violet's. Would I never be free of her? Did I want to be?

Letter from Alice David to Ann St.John
February 11, 1935

Dear Ann,

How are you, dear? I hope you are well. Things were looking terribly bleak here, but some interesting developments as of late have made us hopeful that our plan will come out as we hoped. I'm not certain what, if anything, you have heard from your Luke, and I wouldn't want to jinx our good fortune...but Maxwell and myself have every hope that our little charge will make a recovery. If not a full recovery, then at the very least she will be back to her old self soon.

As far as your concerns about Luke, I am not certain how to address them. I can only use your descriptions on the changes wrought in him as a guide, but it seems that a hollow has descended over many of the pieces of his character that before now held nothing but levity and happiness. Max and I would be deceiving you if we said we did not find him much changed. He is still the same loving, kind person we've grown to love and had hoped would someday call our son-in-law, but there is something altered in his manner, a cynicism, a distrust of those that surround him. Which although is understandable, it is also difficult to watch a shadow like that pass over the life of one so young.

I must also tell you of the strange obsession he has developed with the changes in our poor girl. He has somehow convinced himself that he can cure her by teasing her, mocking her and confusing her. He says that he thinks the challenges are good for her mind. I, for one, can't help but think she has been through enough without being subjected to games.

And, at long last, Violet. I know we both have the same fears concerning the subject of their romance. Although that heartbreaking day was so many months ago, I had hoped that by the time Luke got here that his affections for her would have subsided, or at least the the flames of his regard would have sizzled down to a manageable blaze, but I see now that you were right in your last letter. He still thinks he is deeply in love with her, even though she is-- gone. His feelings have twisted something inside of him, and I'm not sure if he could be reached by anyone. Max has made some efforts to talk to him, to discuss with him the way feelings and relationships can be altered through events and time, but perhaps it is too early yet to expect him to be healed. They were virtually inseparable those six years or so, we can't expect an association and fascination that lasted so long would be so easily quitted. For my part, although I think it is damaging to the boy, I also find it charming that he had/has such high regard for our girl. It says much about his character and the way he was raised.

Ann, thank you for obliging me by allowing me to send you yet another rambling letter of no importance. Your friendship and support throughout...this, has been invaluable to me. God bless you.

Affectionately,

Alice David

Journal

February 14, 1935

It is St. Valentine's Day. Not that this day ever held much for me before. But it does seem depressing to be spending it here.

I had a dream last night, all of my dreams are cold lately. I am either swimming in a sea of ice, or standing on an iceberg watching the heat of my breath enter in and out my nose and mouth like bad spirits escaping from my troubled mind. I can't help but think these dreams are brought on by the ice cold hydrotherapy baths I am continually subjected to. I awake like a child in the night crying out for the arms and comfort of a mother I cannot picture in my mind nor remember. Even the idea of Luke, which used to be a source of comfort to me here in this place, even he has become a source of distrust, a serpent in the garden.

I sense he doesn't want me to be happy. I sense that he doesn't want me to get better. And a thought has crept into my diseased mind these last few days. A very bitter thought. First, I feel that he is hiding something from me. In his presence I feel like he is keeping something from me, he is carrying some secret around with him, itching him and torturing him like a hair shirt. I mean to have it from him, even if it means he will not come to see me anymore. Which, even for all of my distrust and hurt, will be a bitter blow. He is like a light when he visits, and I cannot but help think that there is a string tying my heart to him, and the further he moves away from me, the string tugs on my chest to the point where it is almost painful to the touch. One might think these are the idle fancies of an ignorant girl, insane and mouldering in an asylum, but I mean it truly. He is a connection with the outside world and a light in my day, but I cannot help feeling that he is also a connection to my past, whatever that may be. It would be terrible to lose him, but I cannot tolerate any more secrets or half-truths.

Secondly, I am suspicious of how, when, and for what reason I was placed in this institution. A few weeks ago I was sure of my name, my family, my relationship to Violet and all of that certainty has systematically been destroyed. I look back at old entries within this journal, and I seem a very different type of person than I feel I am today. I was a sad, young woman, best friend to Violet, my parents were anxiously awaiting me back in Chicago, and I was only here because I was suffering from severe depression after the beating, rape and murder of my dear friend. What madness is this? What of my existence between October when she was attacked, and when I came to the asylum this January? Why can't I remember anything? And most frightening, why am I in an asylum, an asylum near the summer home of my dead friend's parents when I am suffering from depression? Should I not be around my own family? Why would someone who is sunken into a pit of melancholia be tucked away into a place so cold, so desolate, so friendless? It's something that one would do if they were trying to make sure that someone sad would never find happiness again.

And that's when I hit on it. There were more lies here. I have been secreted away, made to forget about my own past, and instead reminded daily of Violet. Her things are left here for me to find. Her boyfriend comes here to flirt with me. There is no mirror in my room. I receive no correspondence from my family. My only visitors are people who loved Violet. I am given electric shock treatments which leave me loopy and confused, easily open to suggestion.

It is my sincere belief that they are all entered together on a plan to make me believe that I am Violet. Or at the very least steal my life away from me and create a living doll that may act, speak, dress and look like Violet. Not only have they made me a prisoner here, but I am a prisoner in my own mind as well...for I cannot remember my old life.

Now for the greatest shock of all; I find it not disagreeable to become Violet. But something in me is fighting it. Something deep within me rages at taking on a life that is not mine, there is something about giving up and becoming her that feels wrong and somehow...painful. I have not decided how my conduct towards the David's will be going forward, and I am completely torn about how I should act around Luke. I am not sure I can control my words or feelings around him; he is dangerous for me.

I look now, inside myself for the strength to make sense of all of the threads I have pulled out, that now lay strewn about me, demanding to be ordered and understood.

St. Valentine's Day indeed.

Diary of Luke St.John

February 14, 1935

So, it's St. Valentine's Day, and I've decided to do something special for the young lady in my life. Mrs. David thinks the way I've been treating her is unkind, but they'll all see. In the end, I'll have her all to myself.

Which brings up a few reservations I've been having. Some cards I've held close to my chest these past months that have been tearing me apart. Some details that I know Mr. David found out from the police...my only refuge is in believing that he hasn't shared that news with anyone. When we are discussing things he and I, man to man, I can feel a disappointment in his voice, a change in his manner that was not there before the incident. Not that I can blame him. But, I wish there was a way to make him understand that it meant nothing. I'm young, Violet was young, I had to be sure. It's hard to be away, even if it was just across town at the University of Chicago. She was older, less moody, less flighty, but also less dreamy and sweet. She lived so solidly in my world, I never felt at a loss with her. I felt like the man on top, the guy who pulled the strings. But one night out to dinner and some necking when I took her back to her apartment was enough to tell me I was a damned fool. A fool for sneaking around on Violet. I knew in that moment that all of it was about me. It wasn't her. Violet was the way she was. She's an imperfect mess of a girl that made a mess of me. I liked that. I loved that about her. She was just irresistibly herself all the time, it was intense and sometimes painful to be faced with that much personality constantly. Demanding my attention, demanding that I come to live in that world with her where nothing and everything made sense. But I was a better man for it, and it scared me. Scared me to see how much less I was without her.

How many times can a man admit he's wrong? How many times can I feel ashamed of a mistake? If that stupid nut of a girl hadn't seen me in Lou's that day, maybe I would have run after Violet to walk her home and none of this would have happened. Maybe if I hadn't been in such a rush to get away from her, to get that girl as far away from Violet as possible, then I could have prevented losing the only goddamn thing in my life that meant anything. Maybe I wouldn't be a hollow shell of a coward that is lower than a kicked dog. How can you apologize to a girl who can't hear you or forgive you? How do you get forgiveness when it's too late to be forgiven?

You can't. And Mrs. David's right. What am I doing with myself now besides dropping out of school and taunting a broken girl in an asylum? I heard her cries when I left her room and they made me smile. What kind of person would smile about that? All I could think in my twisted selfishness was, "I've got her feeling something. I'm getting through to her." Why do I hurt the people I love? There must be something wrong with me that I have to stab into the very heart of the trust and kindness of those around me in order to feel better or understood, myself.

Mr. David has only said one thing to me about it. In fact, I can hardly believe I got off so lucky. When I first arrived in Traverse City, after Mrs. David had left us alone for a glass of brandy in his study, he had broken off mid-conversation, looked at me sternly and said simply, "The waitress there at Lou's. She talked to the police you know." I must admit that for a moment I wasn't sure what he was getting at, on account of how often Violet and I snuck off there. It really could have been a number of things that he was referring to. I reddened as a result of my confusion, and he continued on, pretending as if he didn't notice. "That last day. You two didn't leave together. You left with another girl. A girl that seemed upset about something, I gather." My eyes had widened and I could feel sweat beginning to drop down my back. This was more than I had bargained for. I had completely forgotten...it had gotten lost in the more *important events of the day, and as I said before, she really hadn't meant anything to me. She was a diversion, a mistake, a lesson. I had been anxious to forget and move on, to love Violet more completely and purely.*

I, of course, could not say any of this to her father. So I met his eyes like a man, and said "yes, sir." He nodded, as if pleased that I had not deigned to lie about it. He went on, "Son, you're always welcome in this house. And no one here would ever think less of you. But if you have someone back in Chicago that you need to be taking care of, we understand that you don't want to spend time with a confused girl in a hospital. We'd understand. You always have and always will be like family to us, even if you never got to be...officially." He seemed to wince on this last word. Violet and I had been exceptionally lucky. Even though we had an age difference, our families had been such close friends that they had always liked the idea of us getting hitched. This was his way of letting me off the hook. His way of telling me that I could go back to my old life, no strings attached, no grudges held. I could find a nice girl and marry her and live on like it had all never happened.

But it had happened. Knowing and loving Violet was the most exciting, important adventure of my life. One mistake didn't alter that. Turning my back on the memory of what we had been would, to me, be the ultimate betrayal. I refused to be afraid of how I felt, I refused to show the weakness I had showed in betraying her. Some might say that men shouldn't talk this way, or that men don't really feel this way about a woman in real life. And, I'd have to say that any man that can't see the wonders of the woman in front of him is blind and stupid and not any kind of man at all. I know, because I've been that. But when you lose what you hold most dear, you begin to understand its importance...but often we are blind until it is too late. But, it wasn't too late for me to finally step up and be the type of man I could be proud of.

I looked back at him, met his eyes, and told him that there was nowhere else on this earth that I belonged except for where they needed me to be. I knew Mr. David, being a former solider in the Great War, admired directness and blunt truths, and apparently this pronouncement was all he needed to hear, because I haven't heard a word about any doubts or misgivings since.

I have received letters from some of my school chums and friends from my classes at University, pleading me to move on and move forward. They just can't understand that to "move on" would be running away. But I see it, and in the end my own approval will have to be enough.

Although there is nothing specifically romantic or happy to celebrate, I have resolved to bring a little happiness into Traverse City State Hospital today. And perhaps, confess my transgression to my favorite occupant. I have been fighting myself on this decision, trying to see if I am seeking to assuage my own anguish only, or if it might bring some type of resolution of unknown pain to her as well. I must think more of my motives before I decide. I will send a small gift, and then perhaps, I will come up to visit on Saturday, the 16th. Hopefully by then I will have settled my next course in my mind.

I hope that I am able to bring enough smiles with the gift, to wipe away the tears I spread like footsteps on the snow of her cheeks.

Journal

February 14, 1935: Evening

I have finally resorted to writing. I have been so torn apart these past few hours that I did not know what to do with myself. But I also did not want to risk my agitation being overly noticed, as I am in no mood to be drug down into that antiseptic prison of a room and shocked until my brain feels as if it melting into my ears. I had been feeling a little put out about St. Valentine's Day earlier, and could never have imagined how my feelings about it would change as the day went on.

I had been sitting in my room drawing, and although I am no great artist, it brings me focus and clarity and freedom from the tedium of life here. When there was a knock on the door. I had dressed decently smart today on the odd hope that I might have a visitor. But, I was a bit deflated to see no one but the nurse walk in the door. My hopes jumped right back up in rhythm to the wild metronome of my heart when I glanced at her arms to see a bouquet of flowers and a letter. I dashed over and took them from her, and she, bless her, knew enough to take her leave quickly and leave me to experience my gifts in a sugary solitude of happiness. The letter was kind, and complimentary...lightly flirtatious. It spoke of his desire to make me smile, and that he would come in the flesh on Saturday to make sure that the smiles he sent had stayed in place. It did not declare grand passion, but it was sweetly written and sweetly received. The flowers were glorious, and I could not imagine how he possibly had afforded to have them shipped from whatever golden clime he had ordered them from. I held them to me in a kind of embrace, they felt alive and the color was blinding in this tomb of quiet grey, hard walls surrounded by a tossing sea of snow. The most vibrant purple hue, so bright it was almost fantasy. I could hardly believe that such beautiful things grew in the world, and then reflected on how much winter could do to dampen and harden the heart. I was completely open and alive to the moment and felt... like myself, whatever that might mean. When it dawned on me.

I looked at my beautiful bouquet of flowers. The tag that stuck out the top simply said "flower of my heart". But the cogs of my mind were already turning faster and faster. There was something wrong with these flowers. Something hateful. I could feel the urgency of the feeling surge through me until the truth hit right in my heart. I threw them away from me, dashing them to the floor where they scattered like shards of glass. VIOLETS! He had dared to send me VIOLETS! And to flaunt in my face that Violet was the "flower" of his heart! His cold, black, hateful heart. Why does he treat me so? Why does he torture me? I could not have felt more right about my wild beliefs of this morning. I was a toy, a plaything in their machinations. In their sickness they had somehow decided to alter me in the image they wished to see. Far away from anyone who could speak for me, I was helpless. Except that I was on to them.

And so for the second time in not many days I laid under my covers to cry. To grieve that I could never be the object of Luke's affection because I was not and could never be *her*. Anger at myself for part of me wanting to be her, grieving about the hold he had on me that I couldn't understand. Once again tortured for the unremembered life that I believed I must have been happy in.

I have resolved to try and write about some of the things I do remember, even if Violet is in the memories. I will do this in the hope that by exploring these memories some of the truths about who I really am will be revealed to me.

Letter from Dr. Emmett Blanchard to The David Family

February 15, 1935

Dear Sir and Madam,

I am writing to request that you please abstain from visiting until further notice. After an extended interview this morning with the patient, and a consultation with the other doctors in residence, we find that although there have been provocative, and I dare say hopeful, developments in the patient's condition and healing, it is the opinion of this staff that she will require a few days of quiet reflection to achieve the greatest benefit.

Also, after much reflection, it is the decision of this institution not to observe this ban on a young man that I understand to be stopping at your household. The patient has specifically requested that visits from a Mr. Luke St.John be continued as she finds his presence cathartic and calming. Personally, my staff and I have our misgivings about any therapeutic effect his visits may or may not provide, however, because this entire course of treatment is experimental we have decided to allow his visits to continue at this time.

I have been given to understand that he is expected by the young lady at some time in the late morning on the morrow. I will send any further notes or messages by courier to keep you apprised of her condition and of developments.

Thank you for your continued understanding and assistance in this experiment.

Regards,

Dr. Emmett Blanchard, M.D.

Journal

February 15, 1935

I have only just returned from a whirlwind morning. I had a very hopeful interview with Dr. Blanchard, which I will recount momentarily, and then a very interesting stroll through the grounds here at the asylum with my nurse.

I daresay I have begun to feel like she is "my" nurse, because she is the closest thing to a friend that I have. Though she is usually mostly silent when we are together, I receive a sort of silent sympathy from her that I find not unrewarding. Today, for whatever reason, perhaps she sensed the frustration and confused nature of my interview with Dr. Blanchard, perhaps not, but in any case she had much more to say to me than usual. As we walked about grounds, she told me some of the history of the asylum. Originally, and still sometimes, called the Northern Michigan Asylum for the Insane, it was built here in the 1880s. According to the nurse, who's name I have finally found out is Nelle, it took a fair bit of pleading and politics to have the asylum built here. Traverse City was founded on timber like much of the northern parts of the state, and when the town began to see a need for something to replace that economic staple they were ravenous at the chance to have the state's third asylum built up in the wilds of this northern place.

She recited all of the information as if she had learned it by rote, but then paused, and glanced sidelong at me. When I returned her look, she smiled and began telling me a little more about the setup of the hospital itself. It seemed I had guessed correctly when I mused before about how the asylum was set up and sectioned out.The building that I am staying in is called Building 50, my room is in the northern part of the building as this is where all female patients are housed--male housing is in the south of the building. Building 50 is very large and expands outward in a grand fashion ruling supremely over the other buildings that make up the complex here. One of the mottos here at the asylum is "work is therapy" and so even now in the sugar snow covered morning I could see heartier patients trudging out with work implements, goodness knows what they were toiling on. I thanked my lucky stars that however unpleasant my ice baths were, the emotional and physical devastation they reek on my burning gooseflesh, was not equal to the labor done in the merciless northern winter.

The last piece of information she volunteered was that the patients in Building 50 were the most severely *affected* patients.

When I inquired, shocked, if the residents of Building 50, like myself, were dubbed thus because we were more dangerous, more insane or least likely to recover, she stopped mid-step.

"I said, *most severely affected*, did I not, child?", she asked, but in a tone that I could not quite identify. I was still puzzling over what that meant, but decided to approach her response optimistically. Besides, why would she be telling me these details of the hospital if I was a harm to anyone, or so terrifically insane that I could not in any way benefit from the information? No, she was talking to me out of kindness, and I felt that she was sharing these details somehow to assuage my fears or to remove doubts.

We both grew silent, lost in our own thoughts, our feet shuffling along to the music of rustling trees and the whisper of our leather boots through the white sand of winter. Building 50 was beautiful. In a sad, hard kind of way. The way that mausoleums arrest our attention, or a soldier in uniform. Beautiful, but also with a coldness that we are unable and unwilling to connect with. I knew from before I had ever come to live at the hospital that the other phrase associated with the place was "beauty is therapy", and perhaps the architects had felt they had done this axiom justice with the grandiloquent plans and drawings they had drawn up as ideas for the future site. But, in execution, the first impression one had was not of beauty, but of sadness. I am sure many people have come through here, have been cured and returned back to their lives of busy nothings, I hope to one day be one of them. But it is cruel to think because of that fact, that 'hope' would be a resonating feeling. It is not. It is an edifice steeped in sadness, in despair, and consuming madness. I shuddered then, but not from the cold, but instead from the feelings of dread that had begun to eclipse my heart. What if I did find myself shut away in this beautiful prison until the end of my days? Would I ever be well? What exactly was wrong with me? Just how long had I been here?

With this question formed on my paper-dry lips, I turned around to ask Nurse Nelle that very moment. I knew that she knew, and I was fairly confident that she would tell me. Her expression when I turned, though, froze my mouth tightly shut. I was alarmed, but did not show it, instead waiting for her to speak. Her face was twisted up, it seemed in a foiled attempt to prevent crying. I noticed for the first time that Nelle was not too many years older than myself, and quite pretty in a solid sort of way. I still did not speak. Somehow she brought herself back under control, and in lieu of explanation, gestured with her hand, urging me to walk a few paces more while she collected herself. I followed her silent directions in complete bewilderment, unable to imagine what had caused such an emotional explosion in so stoic a young woman.

Less than a minute later, she caught up with me. I slowed my pace to match hers, and suddenly her voice, a rasping flutter of wings, so quiet I had to bend my ear closer to listen, "I am so glad to see how far you have come, Miss. Excuse me speaking out of turn, but you are positively unrecognizable from when you arrived here this past December. None of us nurses had any hope for you, I'm sure. But your face, and your manner--they reminded me of a friend I once had, before the influenza. She and you both had a fire, you see, a fire that had been starved down to a spark. I asked for you, Miss. I told Dr. Blanchard that I would see you well again. He asked me, 'What if she is unable to get well?' I told him right then and there that you *would* get well indeed." At this point in her narrative she stopped and gave my arm a friendly squeeze before continuing, "But he insisted, and I told him that if you couldn't get well, that I would see you happy and comfortable. Now what do you think of that?"

She seemed very pleased with herself. I wasn't sure at all what I thought of that. But I did know now that I had been here since December. Which was troubling to me since I only had recollections since January. She had continued to keep an eye on me though, apparently wanting an answer, and so I told her honestly, "I'm sorry, but I am neither happy nor comfortable". If I had thought that this news would depress her spirits, I was mistaken. She smiled all the broader and said, "Oh, I am glad to hear it. That is because you are getting well!" With that final thought, and no time left to process it, she quickened her pace to move ahead of me and I knew that our walk was at an end. She directed herself toward the doors, and I lagged behind trying to piece together and untangle all of the strings I had been given to hold on to. So focused on these wonderings, my boot slipped on a stone hidden in the snow, and as I steadied myself I looked down to see the concealed green that was underfoot. It reminded me of myself. Somewhere deep down, the real me was buried beneath this facade of mystery. I had bundled myself up in it for the time being, but when I was ready, when my heart and my head readjusted, I would reemerge to the world, like I'd never been gone. The corners of my mouth lifted, and a laugh escaped from my mouth. It was the first time I'd truly laughed in longer than I could remember, the kind of laugh that rolls through your whole body like a wave.

These events though, were secondary to what had happened just before the walk that day. I had risen early, bathed, dressed quickly and requested to speak to Dr. Blanchard as soon as he was available. To my surprise, hardly a moment later the man himself entered my room.

He was a picture of perfect self control and respectability. His duties and professionalism he wore as easily as his spectacles, sitting perched on his nose like a trained bird. He is portly, wears a fatherly face and generally appears as one of those people who genuinely finds themselves performing a task in their life that they enjoy, and whom you could not picture in any other line of work. Yes, Dr. Blanchard was created for dealing with the people that the rest of society couldn't, or preferred not to. It wasn't because he was kinder or more compassionate than other people, it was simply that he was suited for it and never questioned whether he should like to do anything else. The whole idea of his finding satisfaction in another line of work would be appalling and distasteful to him if anyone had ever suggested it, and from the ease of his manner, it was clear no one ever had.

He came in, offered me his customary worried smile reserved for patients, which seemed to say "Oh dear, what's the trouble now?", and taking a seat across from me, he crossed his legs, took out a pad of paper and handsome pen and looked at me down his rather pug-like nose. We discussed small things for a few minutes. How was I feeling? Was I enjoying more exercise? Is anything on my mind? And at the last question, I latched on and seized the opportunity.

I clearly, concisely and in the least hysterical way that I possess, explained to Dr. Blanchard my doubts and misgivings about the motives of the David's. I even intimated that I had a feeling, that if such a thing were true and they were actually trying to brainwash me into believing I was Violet, that he might be in on it too. I only touched on it delicately, and then skipped on to telling him my conflicting feelings about Violet and that I was frightened that I was forgetting more and more of myself. When I came up for air in that drowning confession, I realized I was no longer seated, but at the window.

I lifted my eyes to gaze out at the dark-blue swelling glassiness of Lake Michigan, and out across the wind-torn wilderness of Traverse Bay. I took a few calming breaths, my desire more than anything was to appear rational. I needed him to believe me, I needed him to at least find me reasonable enough to explain *why* I was having these doubts and thoughts. I could not stand to be treated anymore like the silly, broken girl that I know I am. I would make him respect the strength and conviction of my words. Taking my eyes off of the wild scene, just a pane of glass away from freedom, I turned to face him and instantly recoiled in confusion.

He was smiling, and nodding his head. He repeated, "I see, yes. Most interesting. Provocative even...yes." He went on this way for a few more moments, and then locking his eyes on mine, he said that he didn't see any reason why this wasn't true. He agreed, it did seem likely that they were trying to convince me I was Violet. When I asked him then, about my own family, my own identity, he replied, "Ah, my dear, if you haven't a clue, why would I?" I felt my resolve begin to falter, thinking he was playing with me. He could see this in my face, because stepping forward, and raising my wrist as if to check my pulse, he said, "My dear, you have made an excellent case that the David's have ulterior motives in your care here, and that you believe them to have secreted you away from your family as a result of your anguish over, and familiarity with Miss Violet David. I do not disagree with you. But until you begin remembering who you *are* I cannot do anything to prove who you *are not*. If you will believe me, you have received no treatments in this facility that would alter your mind into believing something different from the truth. On the contrary, the therapeutic treatments you have received here at this asylum have only been of a nature to soothe and prohibit hysteria."

He gave me a few moments to process all of this, and the more that I thought, the more that his words rang true. I came to the realization that as much as I hated to admit it to myself, I needed more time. To think, to remember, to grieve, to come back into myself. When I looked back up from my thoughts to meet his gaze, he continued, "As far I am concerned, it would be a good idea for the David's not to visit anymore for a few days. Or anyone for that matter. You may need some time to yourself here, to collect your thoughts. If this is your wish, I will write to them directly."

It was my wish. It was as if he was reading my thoughts. I was elated for a reprieve from the awkwardness of their visits while I was still formulating a plan of behavior in their presence. However, there was one aspect of his suggestion that did not sit well with me, a faint nagging tug under my rib cage. A lightness in my stomach that made me feel slightly light-headed. Slowly sensing the cause of my unease, I sat up straight, and taking a deep breath, hoped that I sounded braver than I felt. "Dr. Blanchard, upon consideration I find your plan well thought out and with every appearance of helping me towards success. Yet, there is one alteration I would like to make. I am most desirous to have a few days without the attentions, whether they are genuine or malevolent, of the Davids, but I cannot find it in my heart or mind to extend this banishment from Mr. St.John. He has shown himself to be an empathetic ear and a touchstone of loyalty since his first visit, and I would be glad for said visits to continue."

Sitting back as though this was the most common sense request in the world, I looked at him, hoping that I betrayed nothing in my expression. Dr. Blanchard, offered a sort of half smile, and patting his knee thoughtfully, said "Quite right. Quite right. A dispensation to the family I had not thought of. It will be less brutal to give them the news this way. Quite right, my girl. A first rate idea." He began to stand up, and then from this upright posture, looked down at me, with I think, some affection. It was apparent that he had something more to impart to me, and so I directed my eyes toward his, still wishing to be considered his equal in sanity and respect. He cleared his throat, and said, "There is a final thought I would like to leave you with, my dear. Though you may have lost your friend, and perhaps for now have lost yourself, if you search hard enough and keep your head about you, I have no doubt of you returning to complete health. That being said, I also want you to think on this: when we experience a trauma, a piece of us dies with it. A small part. A large part. Even our very selves. It is no shame to have lost yourself, temporarily, in the pain of a tragic event."

Without another word, he nodded his head quickly, turned on his heel and walked out the door, closing it securely behind him. I must admit that his speech fairly unnerved me, and as I gazed at the door in complete puzzlement, to my surprise, it popped open once again and in came Nurse Nelle, smiling as if there wasn't a worry in the world to be had by anyone.

Letter to Dr. Emmett Blanchard from Mr. Maxwell David

February 15, 1935: Afternoon

Dr. Blanchard,

I cannot say that I was surprised to receive your note, and I beg that you will forgive my replying so soon and so suddenly. I know that we are all working towards the same goal, namely the full recovery of the young woman we have entrusted to you.

That being said, I am urged by my wife to inquire as to the length of our banishment from the facility. As you well know, this has been a horrifying past year for my family, and my wife especially has been bent and broken by her powerlessness over the situation. Your letter was a bitter blow to us, Dr. Blanchard and we are a family that has weathered far too many in the recent past. If possible, could you please offer us a rough estimate until we may be welcome to visit again?

Although deeply troubled that we are not wanted, we were glad that our patient does continue to want to receive visits from Mr. Luke St.John. His continued influence over her has been a beacon of hope for us, and for our plans for her. I fear that the visits are difficult for him to bear, however, and I am unsure if he will find himself able to continue them. If you are at leisure tomorrow when he visits, I wonder if you could perhaps explain to him just how our experiment is progressing and why we felt it necessary. I fear that his misunderstanding of our motives have proved troubling to him, and have caused no small amount of pain.

We continue to be guided by your good sense and judgement and still earnestly hope for a recovery. I have sent this message with one of the boys who works in the house. I have given him leave to travel between here and the asylum several times a day to deliver messages back and forth if necessary, in order for us to keep our contact discreet and swift.

Regards,

Maxwell David

Journal

February 16, 1935

Luke visited today, and again I find that
I am completely mystified as to how to
describe the experience. Even before he arrived
late in the morning, I was an octopus of
emotion. Each tentacle representing a different
feeling and each swimming in different ways,
so that I felt as if I might simply pull apart. I
had many opposing forces preying on my
mind.

First, the violets. The gesture had so
elated me until I realized the type of flowers.
His note made me certain that the flowers were
not chosen subconsciously or by happenstance.
The thought behind it all had stirred
something deep within me. Not only physical
desire, but a desire to connect with *him*. Not
because I have been devoid of real human
connection here, although that is certainly true
too, but something deeper, almost tangible. I
feel myself tied to him, like an anchor to a ship.
His presence somehow, as awkward and
befuddling as his visits have been, has kept me
floating aloft instead of drowning in misery
and the confusion of myself and my presence
here in this hospital.

When he arrived, consequently, I did not quite have the presence of mind for the conversation. He opened the door, painfully punctual, and seemed to glide in like a wave to the shore. He smiled pleasantly, removed his hat and put it in his lap, and then sat back crossing his legs. He smiled, looked down at his cream marled sweater and adjusted it for a moment. I daresay he could feel my nervousness, and he was deciding on how to react to it. Or perhaps this is my imagination and he was nervous too. Nervous why though? Why would *he* be nervous around *me?* Surely he had no reason to feel awkward unless he did not wish to be visiting me at all. Fighting back these doubts and negative thoughts, swallowing them down and choking on them like a mouth full of sea water, I finally brought myself to meet his gaze.

In his eyes I found only kindness. He looked at me expectantly, as if he had been looking forward to hearing me speak and was pleased now that I was ready to do so. I felt the shadow of a smile creep onto my face. In a single moment I was buoyant, no longer sinking. He then asked me if I had received his gift, and with a shadow creeping into my chest, I replied that I had. He seemed to be waiting, and I winced as I told him that although it was thoughtful and touching, I feared it may have been an inappropriate gesture. His eyes searched mine, as if he could plunge the depths of them and find the answer without having to ask me anymore about it. Not wanting to encourage the intimacy, (but also wanting to fall into it completely) I decided to enlighten him.

"Luke, I am not Violet." as soon as the words left my mouth and the sound of them was still reverberating in the room, I wondered to myself if it had been the right thing to say. It felt right, and it felt wrong at the same time. All of my thoughts came to a screeching halt, like a trolley flying wildly off the track, when I saw his expression. He cleared his throat, pulled his hand through the brown waves of his hair, exhaled quickly, and looked back at me. "I know that. It's just that...that...we both miss her. I thought. I thought that purple was your favorite..." He added the last part lamely, almost as an after thought. I explained that no, that purple was Violet's favorite, and that anyway, his note had made it perfectly clear whom he wanted to be giving the flowers. He looked back, eyes piercing into mine, when all of a sudden, an amused look came to his face. He had gained back his equanimity. "All right then, missy. If purple *isn't* your favorite, perhaps you could enlighten me as to what *is*."

He had won, and he knew it. Because as hard as I tried to think, I didn't know. All I could see was purple now that we had talked about it so much. I saw visions of violets and amethysts and periwinkle sunsets. Of lavender fields and ripe plums and lush mauve blankets covering me head to foot as I curled up in a bed I didn't remember but knew was either my imagination or a memory. I tried to cling to the memory for a moment and see what else it would reveal, but my thoughts simply swirled around in shades of a purple sea. I shrugged and told him he was right, I was in no position to tell him what I liked or didn't, who I was or wasn't. Instead of being pleased, he looked crestfallen.

He shook his head, muttering apologies. I reached forward to take his hand in mine, needing to feel a closeness to this handsome man before me. This man that I knew but did not know. This man that I loved, but could not love, for he was in love with a girl who was dead, buried, young and beautiful and perfect forever. A dream girl that died rather than become this bent and withered feather of a person. Still I reached out, wishing to show him that I was not really angry, just hurt and confused. Hoping to communicate the swarm of my feelings through the touch of my skin on his. At the last moment, he flinched from my touch. Even as I write this, I cannot explain the depth of that pain, the betrayal of my feelings in that moment. I was drowning, just about to reach the life preserver that had been thrown to me, and at the last moment it had been jerked mercilessly back into the boat, leaving me slowly treading water.

He looked at me in agony. These moments are so simple, and may to an outsider have seemed trivial, even boring; but to one who has undergone the sheer emotional turmoil with feelings unexpressed and doubt and fear of the next words that would tumble from someone's mouth. If one has felt that way, one knows there is more adventure, more drama, more excitement in a single glance than in a hundred brave actions. The human heart can burst so much more easily from a moment like this, than from the excitement of shooting out of a cannon or climbing a tall mountain. Life is mostly comprised not of using the right verbs, but in choosing the correct adjectives.

Finally speaking, he said he had to make a confession to me. Trying to make light of the moment, I told him I was no priest, and that I could not play his confessor. I smiled, hinting towards playfulness, but his face remained impassive. I realized instantly that although he had lately in visits been given to short bouts of sadness, that he wasn't usually one for theatrical displays of seriousness. A little apprehensively, I told him I would be glad to listen to anything he had a mind to share, and sat forward in my chair. He asked then if I minded taking our conversation outside, that it was unnerving him to stare into my eyes. I quickly agreed and after a very few minutes of outfitting ourselves for the cold winter air, we emerged outside into the noonday sun. It felt almost hot outside under all of my layers with the sun beating down savagely on the top of my head. In my haste I had forgotten to cover it with a hat. I was so eager though, that Luke should continue, I made no mention of it. Instead I linked my arm in his, hardly thinking of the impropriety, if there was any, of the action.

He started speaking quickly, once we were outside. His stride was easy, and somewhat slower than normal. He was talking, but for a moment I didn't realize it was to me. His usually animated voice sounded, flat, lifeless. As if he were speaking from the bottom of a well. He was saying something about a girl. A girl that meant nothing to him. He told me how he had courted her, and held her hand, how he had kissed her passionately and willed her to be Violet. I didn't understand his words. Was he talking about me? When had this happened? He looked at me, his eyes begging me to understand. Seeing the utter bewilderment on my face, he began again to explain. He spoke of a girl that he had met at the University of Chicago, a girl that looked a bit like Violet. Again I was lost in his words, trying to make sense of what he was so earnestly trying to tell me. He had been unfaithful, he said.

Finally. It hit home. Luke St.John had been unfaithful to Violet. Violet who loved him passionately and beyond measure. It hit me hard in the gut, but I couldn't tell you why to save my life. I had imagined before that to Violet, Luke may have been special, but she didn't really have time to be tied down. This was probably what she had thought herself. With those words though, that silly notion was toppled. Violet would never have tied herself down to just anyone, she had completely loved Luke, she had trusted him. She was dead and he had been unfaithful to her.

It made me shake. I felt myself quivering, the heat of the day seemed to have disappeared, behind a dark cloud. My hands were ice, my stomach had dropped, I felt like I might be sick. I wasn't angry at Luke, though. I couldn't explain that either. I wasn't upset with him, but with Violet. She was always *so much*. I could feel that others around her had a hard time living, really living the way she did. Savoring each moment, not giving a good goddamn what anyone else thought. Dreaming the biggest, laughing the loudest. It had been too much for Luke, and perhaps too much for me. No one could be filled with so much light and not blind those around them.

He was waiting for me to say something. I asked him if he had ever loved her. His answer was quick, and I thought, sounded decisive. "I've always loved her. I will always love her. Our souls are attached one to the other. I will love that girl with my entire heart forever, through life and death". It was unsettling. I asked him how he could have been unfaithful to someone whom he felt that way about. "I was a prize idiot. I didn't know what to do with all of the love I had, and all of the love I was getting. It was unnatural to be so out of control. But I realized that being *in control* of anything in life is the only thing that is truly unnatural." I felt, to a degree, recovered. I knew he meant it. And I don't know why he confessed it all to me, but I think, by the end we both knew that he needed to. We walked on silently, in a more relaxed state of mind for a few minutes. I felt the warmth begin to refill my fingers and toes, my body coming slowly back to life from the icy shock of an unwanted truth. As we were heading in, I felt that we had crossed over something together just now. Some barrier or bridge that needed to be traversed, and we had done so. Just one thing more had stayed wriggling in my mind. "Luke, I understand how deeply you love Violet. I can't help but think that she stays within me the same way somehow. But, now that she is gone, do you think you could ever love someone else? Even just a little?" He smiled at me, choosing his words carefully. "Violet David is the love of my life. But, there is someone, who although different from my Violet, who I find increasingly on my mind, and whose company I have come to look forward to very much. Even if it sometimes is a bit awkward". Our eyes met then, and I knew it was myself he was talking about. A seed of hope had been planted, watered and I was urging it to grow. Maybe, just maybe we could both grow to love and accept this person that I was, this lost and found person that I have become.

Diary of Luke St.John

February 16, 1935

Well, I did it. I told her all about it. At first I thought that perhaps it was the wrong thing to do. As the words tumbled from my mouth like so many raindrops in a storm, the deluge almost seemed to assault her. The walls she began to build around herself were palpable, and just when I thought to begin backpedalling over my words, the walls tumbled down, as if they had never been up.

I don't know why, and I don't care, I'm simply glad that it's over and done with. To think that I had made a mess of things before I even showed up too. I can't imagine what I was thinking sending her violets. One track mind I suppose. Why can't I seem to stop throwing Violet in her face? Flaunting my feelings for her, talking about her, saying her name. It's sick. Not for the first time, I felt today that I'm the one who should be in that hospital.

But, there's something else. I told her today of my undying love for Violet, and that remains true. Yet...yet, when I see her smile. The lighting up of her face, the excitement that I've come to visit... well I would be lying if I said there was nothing there. I know in my heart she's not the same. I know to my core that the girl that I loved so dearly is gone forever, and as much as my heart mourns her loss... it can't but brighten at the very thought of this other. It can hardly be considered unfaithful, can it? She is so alike, but then so different than my Violet. I'll have to think on it.

I weary of the days here. Never ending cold, bitter winds, endless days working at the bank, and awkward dinners with the Davids- made even more uncomfortable by the recent letter from the good doctor. I thought Mrs. David was going to have a fit, but she brought her emotions under control. I can't imagine what I've done to make my presence a pleasure to our patient, I feel that more than ever I have made myself a nuisance, alternating between brooding melancholy and vindictively teasing her emotions.

As bleak as things seem here sometimes, if I give myself a good think about being back in Chicago for a few minutes, my intention deepens. This is my place, this is where I can do some good. I have had a letter from my parents back home, and they, unsurprisingly, want an answer about school. I have resolved to return for the fall. Although they have been very kind and understanding during all of this, I cannot bear to let them

*down--I must finish my education and make
something of myself.*

*So strange how insignificant the
problems of the past appear in comparison to
the catastrophic calamities of the past six
months or so. Worrying about which firms to
work for after I graduate, trying to save face
in front of the fellas when they'd give me hell
about being so stuck on Violet, all of this
business with that other girl, all so
meaningless. My mind is so full now, full of
pictures, glimpses of events. They run
continuously, a whirlpool of memories and
some of the images I know are not my
memories, but my fevered imaginings. One
moment I'm sitting in class, taking notes and
fighting sleep, the next moment my hand is
tracing the creaminess of Violet's leg, tugging
off her stockings like the untying of a bow.
Her fresh face a beaming sun ray of happiness
and giggles, the heat of the moment rushing to
her cheeks. I rush from that moment to an
image that haunts me. A juxtaposition of
nightmarish fantasy of a memory that I do
not possess. Me, tugging the girl, Elizabeth
her name was, out of Lou's, and at the same
time I see in my mind's eye the attack on
Violet. I know I wasn't there, but I have
assigned the invented memory as a
punishment. Her cries, her need for me, and
my not being there. I see her blood pooling in
the alley. I see the man, the monster, ravaging*

116

a girl, a woman, that I had cherished beyond measure. I had always stood in awe of her beauty, her form, her intelligence, finding myself not her equal in any of them. But this, unnatural thing did only seek to steal my darling away from me; to steal her soul, to break her body, to kill her spirit. She was a body to be defiled, she was nothing to him.

I cannot justify this in my mind. Not the act, that is without question. But, I cannot square the Violet of my mind and the Violet that he saw. How could anyone be faced with her and not see her worth? How is it possible for any human being to do that to another? I'll never understand it, and I think it's probably a good thing that I can't. A little bit of us all died that day. A part of everyone that loved her. I'm sincerely surprised we're not all in the asylum. Ahh, but I've said that a fair number of times before now, haven't I?

What's next for me? Well, I will write back to my parent's directly. I will go and visit the asylum again in a few days, and for now I will attempt to train myself to not be so concerned with "the next" of everything for a little while.

Letter from Alice David to her brother Arthur,

February 18, 1935

Dearest Artie,

I hope this letter finds you and your family in good health. I have, myself, been in very low spirits lately. While there is word from the hospital that they are in high hopes for our girl, I cannot help but feel that a door to my own Violet has somehow closed forever.

I have been spending time lately thinking. It feels as though that is the premier occupation of everyone in this household lately. Pondering, thinking, dreaming, reminiscing. We are all strapped firmly looking backwards. As if we are all on the back of a boat, only peering over the stern watching the ripples of water that have already been passed over. I miss my little girl, Artie. I miss not watching her become a woman. I miss her twirling around the house and stealing my pearls. I even miss finding the stolen pearls in her room as she vehemently denies ever taking them or seeing them before. She was so full of life. It is unbelievable that a spirit that strong could be snuffed out.

If it wasn't for Max, I would have fallen apart myself. We never speak of what happened to her. We never speak of the attack. I know that it was you and he who first saw her, saw the shattering that had been done to her body. I don't know how either of you could bear it. I can't bear to think of it. I do not know how I will stand to face that monster in court, I do not think that I have the strength. But then I think, Violet would have done it for me. Violet would have faced down anyone for those she loved. She was... intrepid. That's the word that comes to mind. Although, if you were to see the wreck your sister has become, you would wonder how a woman such as me created such a marvel, but, I will continue to hold that she belonged to no one but herself. She loved fiercely, was brutally honest, and it breaks my heart to be without her.

You asked in your last letter about Luke St.John. Yes, he is staying here with us. He's been brave too. I sense a secret within him, perhaps many. I shouldn't wonder too much what they are, young men's secrets are nearly always the same. His mother is forever asking me if he will return to dear old Chicago, and I think he will. But right now, he is held here with us, stuck in another time, aching over things that cannot be changed.

I do not know if we will ever return to Chicago. A mist hangs over that metropolis, and even the friendliest of everyday sights that I recall hold a sort of foreboding or chill for me. The winter is cold here, and there is not much remaining in the area but some timber, and this asylum. The women are kind, though nosy. Besides, we have our responsibilities here, responsibilities we are more than happy to nurture, love and protect.

Please do come visit in the summer. Shall we say June? Your presence is always a salve to me, Artie, and in the meantime your letters are almost as good.

All my love,

Alice

Journal

February 18, 1935

One day drips endlessly into the other. Life at the asylum is painfully regimented for most of the inhabitants, but not for me. Still, it has become a kind of habit for me to watch everyone milling about, moving with the precision of those who are following orders, submitting themselves to authority. It is not that I think myself their superior, on the contrary, I find my own presence of mind almost a failing. It doesn't belong here. Not that everyone at the asylum is so far gone, or deranged. Some people seem pleasant, normal (whatever that signifies) even friendly. I cannot allow myself to be friendly back. It concerns me that once I let go of my will to be different and act different that I will lose my ability to act "normal" and, in effect, ever get well. The doctors and nurses are kind, and no one has felt a need to subject me for treatment of any kind since my chat with Dr. Blanchard...but more than ever I feel like a dolphin in a net. Wriggling, pressing myself against the ropes holding me in...almost convulsing to free myself.

The last few days. I have fished the depths of my mind, searching for my past memories. Casting my own nets out to trap any

loose memories, images, sounds, scents...
anything. I have not come up empty, but my
catch of the day was a jumble of all of these
sensory details, almost more difficult to sift
through...though I daren't throw any back. One
never knows what might be the key to
unlocking my past. Just ordinary things, Violet
laughing or brushing her hair, the exhilaration
of walking into the world's fair in Chicago, the
smell of coffee at night, a paper cut from
turning the pages of a book too quickly. The
sound of a man's laughter, my heart beating
within my chest, some lost old record playing
lazily in another room, the feel of the lake
water dripping off my skin, splashing around
as the wind and water work together plaiting
knots in our hair. Yes, always Violet. She
surrounds me. Her scent, her laugh, her
heartbeat. She is still here haunting me every
time I walk into the room. In the echo of my
own laughter I hear hers, in the lines of my
own smile her feline grin smiles back. She
obsesses me, or possesses me or some mixture
of both. Sometimes the idea of her makes my
thoughts bold and my tongue loose. I say
whatever I please, and sometimes say things
just to shock the nurses that come into my
room.

Other times, I recognize her working on
me and I push her back. I push her back down
and cast out her influence. Calling up my
memories though, has done nothing to retrieve

my own past, but instead has become a path to a deeper fixation on the charmed life of Violet David. I shouldn't say charmed, there is a fair amount of angry outbursts in my memory of slammed doors, and secrets. I find, on reaching back that Violet must have known about Luke's indiscretion after all. Because I realize that even before his confession the other day, I already knew it. I remember the sound of her tears falling like snowflakes. She tried so hard to hold them back, but her heart had turned so cold that in a matter of moments we were both of us, lost in a blizzard of her heartache. I remember her writing a note, in my mind, a cruel note, and having it delivered to an "Elizabeth" and knowing implicitly that she was simply sewing up a loose end.

Had she been angry with Luke? Terribly. Bitter too. But she, how does the poem go?, "Loved with a love that was more than love". Even in her fury of betrayal she wouldn't have given him up. Memories of her endlessly searching for a sign, a sign that he still loved her. Then I remembered, the last day. The day when...it happened. She was going to meet Luke, and she was going to say something so lovely, so gorgeous to him... and his reaction would prove if he was still hers. She was a plotter, a planner. She was sly and cunning and jealous. The memories of her lost life swept over me in a tornado, a swirling chaos of movement, of highs and lows and fears of flying and the double fear of dropping suddenly. Worse yet, when the tornado of reminisces passed over, I was left with the aftermath. A jumble of memories, images and thoughts that were not mine and yet somehow were because I had shared them. I wondered if Luke's reaction at their meeting had given her the confirmation she needed of his feelings.

I wondered too, about her last moments. For the first time in a long time, since before I came in here for my breakdown, I let my mind run over the scene of her death. Why? I felt that if I could understand it, then it would punish me no longer. I knew, somehow, that shutting my mind to her attack had shut it off from the world. I had been told where it had happened, it had been in the newspaper. I had even read the words the reporter had used to describe the rape and subsequent battery before someone had found me with the periodical and taken it away. Where had that happened? Who had taken it away? I couldn't remember that. My imagination filled with blood on the pavement, those same honey locks that had been pulled by a silver brush were stuck on the wall with that same blood. Her dress was torn, and her face, her beautiful face was unrecognizable. It was a contused mass of lumps and blood. I paused my imaginings to find that my face was wet with tears and an awful moan of agony was coming from my mouth. I sat for a while, hugging myself, seeming to crawl deeper and deeper into my own anguish. As I rocked my body back and forth, I was reminded of the soothing motion of the lake. That damned lake kept creeping into my mind. It bridged my old life in Chicago over to this one here in Northern Michigan. The lake, to me was healing. All of it's memories were pure, untainted. A kind of baptism of solace was found in recalling it. It was somehow comforting to think it had always linked the two places together, long before I needed it to, or before it meant anything to me. I thought of seasons past. Of being on the Chicago shorelines and dreaming of the summer trip here, and of finally retreating up here in the summer and looking across the bay towards Chicago, knowing my life was right there where I left it, just across the stretch of blue.

Wiping my tears on my sleeve, I smoothed down the front of my dress. It was navy blue with a light blue pattern that almost looked like waves. I stood up at the thought, at the same time relieved and frightened to be surrounded by so much water all the time. The white frozen snow, the water in the bay, the water that would pour from my eyes at the moment a memory was too much to handle. I brushed my hair back, as my feet automatically made their way towards my window. The sky was clear, and I looked out wanting to be sure that the lake was still there. A touchstone, a token to cling to.

I hit upon an idea then. I'm not sure why or how, but my mind began to form an objective. I would go down to the water. I would escape from here, and I would go down there. I knew it was raw and wintry, especially down by the chilled lake with it's unrelenting winds. Believe me, I have no design to destroy myself, enough death has plagued those around me. I just want to feel myself at peace. To commune with a place that is free from pain, and that is guaranteed to spring to life with warmth and sunshine, even if now it was cloaked in the diamond ice of winter.

When? When shall I go? I do not know yet. I am not convinced it is wise, but it feels right. I feel like I belong near that shoreline. Perhaps I should tell Luke, or have him meet me, although, I am not entirely convinced he would agree to come. When he visits, mayhap I could drop a few hints and see if he puzzles it out himself. Yes, that will do nicely. See how well he has grown to know my moods, it is not my wish to give away my plans, but it would be interesting if Luke were able to join me.

Will I run away from here for good? Will I return after my escapade? I don't have a plan. And yet, it is a relief to make this decision. It is deeply liberating to not know what will come next. To be free from worry or expectation, to know that the steps I take may lead me closer to myself-that is a kind of hope that cannot be found, sitting stagnant in this place.

Diary of Luke St. John

February 20, 1935

All is lost.

I am writing to clear my thoughts, to process through the news we have received this morning. When I went to see her yesterday, she looked well, almost like her old self. She was strangely animated though, and I must admit that I was unsure if I should accept this as a sign that her mental state is more, or less, balanced. There was a secret frenzy of her eyes, an excited glow to her cheeks.

When I first arrived this change in her manner caused me to feel hopeful, but then I realized that her mind wasn't really on me, or on the visit for that matter. Instead of delving in, and trying to figure out her secret, I instead, selfishly, tried to alter the course of the conversation to us. It is the senior preoccupation of my mind, and like a child, I always find myself tugging her dress, begging for answers. I will say it once again, I am a fool. It is because of that foolishness that I have lost her.

She has escaped from the asylum. She has only been out for some six hours, but it was enough to send us into frenzy. We haven't the faintest idea where she could be. My manager at the bank downtown has very kindly given me leave to search for her, but at this point it seems she has disappeared without a trace. We have checked "Hobo Point" out on Boardman Lake's shore, where there is a group of beggars and other "gypsies" living. We have checked the Park Place Hotel, although I for one do not know how a young woman with no identification or money could have gained access. The local orchards, though frozen, have been combed through. The Davids are in hysterics, and I cannot deny that it has thrown me into a panic that I know not how to escape from. How could she? But then again, how could we?

I have lived, all of these months, knowing what we were doing to her. I felt in my heart that this experiment was causing more disease to her mind than cure. Yet, I said nothing. So, I am not only a fool, but a coward. I should have told her. Perhaps she wouldn't have believed me. Maybe it would have caused her to run away before now, or God forbid, take her own life. The truth is such a sticky thing, start dabbing around in it, and it's all over your hands--and it was that above everything that made everyone involved stay away from it. We had to go through with the experiment. She could not be told the truth, at any cost, until the timing was right. But, the timing had never been right.

I have been racking my brains for some clue, some hint in our conversation from that last visit. Some indication of her impending flight, some small implication of where she was going...and that she wanted me to find her. Could I have mistaken the look in her eyes, the desire in her movements? I would have sworn a thousand times that she was feeling the same way for me that I felt for her. That she had remembered me. I have one idea, although I am almost terrified to chase it down. How could she possibly survive in this cold? True, it has been warmer these past few days, almost like spring, but I cannot think she would have made her way toward the lake. Surely, it is an impossibility. The thought nags at me, pulling me forward. I feel somehow that this has to be right. It is true that she has had a strange fascination with Lake Michigan. She speaks in riddles, all of her words sloshing and flowing together like water in a pail. They seem to travel in a vortex of meanings and references, a combination of the life she doesn't remember and the one she wants to build now.

I know now that I must attempt this. I will try and see if I can track her footsteps, or her thoughts. Time is running short and I must make haste. I mean to follow my instincts, and if she is not there, then I pray that somehow I will be led to her. If she is down there by the frigid water, heaven forbid, I pray that she had her wits about her when she planned her escape, and perhaps thought enough to bring something to keep herself warm.

My darling, my girl, my love. How can my heart break when it is already in shards?

Interview with Maxwell David as recorded by:

Sgt. Christopher O'Noulain, Chicago Police

November 1, 1934

Sgt. O'Noulain: Mr. David, could you please give us a summary of events from the moment your family realized your daughter, a Miss Violet Penelope David, was missing to the present moment.

Maxwell David: On October 30, around six o'clock in the evening, my wife and I became aware that our daughter, Violet, had not returned home. We urgently asked around, inquired of our housekeeper when the last time she had been seen was, and then waited. I...

Sgt. O'Noulain: Excuse me, sir, but was it unusual for your daughter to be out without you or your wife's knowledge of her whereabouts? I'd like to have this all clarified for the record.

Maxwell David: It wasn't usual or unusual. Violet didn't often go out without telling us, but she had been known to slip away for an hour or so. We figured she was perhaps meeting a friend at a shop, or meeting up with her sweetheart, a boy who is friends with the family. Around seven o'clock, her beau rang for her at the house, and after a moment of speaking to him, we found that none of us had any idea where she was. By this time I had an awful feeling that something wasn't right. So I phoned the police.

Sgt. O'Noulain: In my report it says that a police officer at the station, a Martin Bradshaw, informed you that a female matching that description had been found, and was en-route to the hospital. Is that correct?

Maxwell David: Yes, sergeant. My wife and I were relieved, that she had been found, and we, hurried to the hospital with all haste, we didn't even ask any of the particulars on the phone. When we arrived, my wife was asked to stay in the hall. The doctors carefully tried to prepare me for my daughter. I must admit, I didn't fully apprehend the gravity of the situation. Who could? How does anyone understand that happening?

Sgt. O'Noulain: What exactly did you see, Mr. David?

Maxwell David: When we got into the room, there were nurses and doctors scrambling around so quickly I could barely make sense of what I was seeing. Except that there was blood. Blood everywhere. My brother-in-law, Arthur entered the room at about this same time, and I remember that we both just stared, trying to make sense of the picture in front of us. I don't think we were supposed to be in the room, but in the confusion we had been let in. As they peeled the remnants of her torn dress away, angry purple spots were already forming all over her pale skin. I knew in that moment that she had been raped. There was so much blood. That antiseptic white room filled with the earthy, rust of blood. My daughter's blood. I realized for the first time, that people can't lose that much blood. That, my daughter might die. She might already be dead.

Sgt. O'Noulain: I'm sorry, Mr. David. I know this is not an interview you wanted to grant, but we need to make sure we gather all of the facts from everyone who saw your daughter before, and immediately after she was admitted into the hospital. We are still piecing together the events of that evening, and we hope to be in touch as soon as we have more answers. Thank you for all of your information, any detail could be invaluable to finding this criminal.

Extract from the notebook of Maxwell David

November 20, 1934

I have much to say, but find I cannot burden Alice with it. It is strange that this notebook, given to me by my wife as a present, within which she had hoped I would disencumber the daily stresses of my professional life, has instead become my refuge from the events of my personal life. Will I ever forget my daughter's unseeing, glassy eyes in the hospital bed? The angry black bruises covering her lovely face? The knowledge that my beautiful, darling girl had been violated and beaten and treated as though she was nothing more than a piece of refuse to be used and then thrown down and forgotten.

It is intolerable. Seeing her on that slab of a bed, her skin cool... too cool. Instead of a vibrant, shining star, she had become a creature of darkness and cold and silence. I weep for my daughter, and I weep for myself.

But, she is alive. If one can call it that. To have your eyes open, and not see everything happening around you. To be touched, and only recoil from the caresses of those that you love. She abhors light. This child of the sun, and of color and smiles... this angel of mine... pulls back when her darkness is intruded upon. She will never have children, she will bear a scar that curves from under her earlobe to the middle of her chin for the rest of her life. The doctor's say the scar will look less cruel in time. That it should heal well.

To imagine, that someone could crack my daughter's face that forcefully into a wall that it tore her skin away from her face is unimaginable to me. I am literally not able to imagine the man who did that, and yet I have seen him. From across the police station. The police have shown me his confession. I am filled with an anger so violent that I cannot believe it could exist within me without tearing me apart. He has stolen our daughter from us. He has said to the police that he had "rather hoped she had died"! I can hardly write for fury. I would see the man dead myself. I would strike out at him with all of the pieces of my ravaged soul...but, but... there is Violet. And Alice. It has been through my duty and love for my girls that I force myself to be contained. That I prohibit myself from acting out my vengeance.

The doctors tell us that her body is healing, slowly, but surely. With time, care and love she will mend. Her mind, however, is something different altogether. It has been difficult for me these past 17 years or so, to watch my daughter grow up. Not in the traditional sense, for I am not the type of father who seeks to rule their daughter. I say it has been difficult because it was obvious to me that my girl would have had a much easier time in this world had she been born a boy. Her mind was always so quick and keen. She could slice through false logic with a knife and laugh in the face of anyone who thought they knew better than she did. I was proud of her. I was proud to have a daughter that thought deeply and had such a unquenchable thirst for knowledge. It is a rare thing for a parent to discover that their child has little to learn from them, it had always seemed that she belonged to herself alone.

Not to say that she was extraordinarily intelligent, or genius. She wasn't. But her personality was so strong, so defined, that it was obvious that she had a deep spirit. The type of daughter that one doesn't worry about too much, as she so obviously has big plans for herself. I was wrong. I should have done a lot of things differently. Because she is lost to us now. She doesn't seem to know us. She doesn't seem to know herself, or even be aware of what is happening around her.

The most devastating part of all of this, the part that I cannot bear to tell Alice, is that I know that Violet chose this.

Yes. Chose. And that is why I have finally broken down and decided to write. For fear that in my grief I will reveal all to her mother, and cause even more sadness. I cannot bear anymore tears to fall than already are all around me. I was sitting in her hospital room, and she was just sitting there, as she has been since she was first admitted. Awake, but not aware. There, yet far away. The door cracked, there was a faint, hurried knock as if whoever was at the door had been in great haste to come in and then realized at the last second that they must knock or seem impolite. When I quietly called out for the visitor to come in, Luke pushed the door open, and stood in the doorway, as if awaiting my further permission. I've always loved the boy. He's a son to me, and I like to think of myself as a second father. We never pushed the two of them together, but from the moment his family moved into town and they met, he was like a planet orbiting around the sun that was Violet.

I gave him a weak smile, and he came in with yet another bouquet of flowers. I would guess that he had cleared out all of the purple flowers to be found in greater Chicago. He had brought a book with him, and asked if it would be alright if he read to her. I saw that it was a copy of "Wuthering Heights" and I winced knowing that although it was a favorite, it clearly centered around love, madness and death. He sat down and began reading, and as his voice sailed smoothly over the words I couldn't help but see that he looked unkempt and careworn. I had only thought of my pain and that of my wife. It occurred to me then that not many twenty year old young men, with their whole lives ahead of them, would spend their afternoons reading and visiting catatonic, broken young ladies. I was touched by his regard for her, but I also wondered how long he would keep it up. Surely, he would tire of it and find someone else.

As my mind was tracing over the probable inevitability of this pain to come, a movement stirred my attention. Violet had reached over, and grabbed his hand as he was reading. I watched her hand interlinking with his, and heard the words from the novel as he read, that have come now to seem to me a kind of prophecy:

"Two words would comprehend my future - death and hell: existence, after losing her, would be hell."

At this point, he looked right into her face, and to my shock, her eyes were no longer unseeing, but instead were as alert and alive as I had ever seen them. She was looking right at him, peering into his eyes, his soul, looking *at the reflection her own ravaged face had on his features. Not by any fault of his own, bless him, but I think she saw something there she didn't like. Pity? Sympathy? Perhaps she thought she saw a slight aversion to her wounds. Whatever it was, I observed her squeeze his fingers one last time, and her face seemed to take on a mask of resignation, and then like a flame burning out, the lifeless expression and pallor returned to her face.*

I saw the change, as did Luke. He was hopeful and thought perhaps we should see her come out of her shell more and more often, but I knew differently. I knew she had detached, that part of her had left. Perhaps never to return. I meet with the doctor tomorrow to discuss these events, but I will never tell Alice. She will be led to believe that she never came out of her trance. I know in my soul that to tell her otherwise would be to rupture my family even more deeply.

Doctor's Observation Notes

December 1, 1934

With some reservations, I have committed to an experimental therapy with a young female patient who after a violent attack, seems to have disassociated from her former self. At this time she does not respond when spoken to, and in short, suffers from Catatonia. According to the reports and interviews with her parents and close friends, she had not been given to melancholia prior to the event of her attack.

The reports from the hospital show a devastating amount of violence done to her person, and in my opinion it is not difficult to see why the mind has chosen or been forced, to detach itself from the realities of the present.

I have gained permission from the family to conduct an experimental treatment. The father has confessed to me that he believes the condition to be in some part, the choice of the patient, made to protect herself. I have taken that information and all others pieces of her case, and decided that it is in her best interest to perhaps, lead her on a path of correcting herself.

She has been described as having an above average mind, and keen self-awareness. In keeping with these strengths, the position of this hospital is that this patient is being treated here for melancholy and not schizophrenia, even though she exhibits catatonic symptoms.

To protect the experiment, her name will not be entered into the hospital books, and the auxiliary staff of nurses and orderlies will be given a fictitious name, in addition to being ordered not to refer to her by any name at all.

We will proceed over the next six months with this alternative treatment, at which time, the experiment will have to be abandoned and the patient will begin regular psychotherapy. My colleagues and I will be working closely to monitor and measure progress.

Emmett Blanchard, M.D.

Traverse City State Hospital

Diary of Luke St.John

December 8, 1934

She is now far away.

*In truth, she has been absent from me
for some time, she never spoke nor showed
that she knew I was near. Her parents have
taken her up to an asylum by their summer
home on the other side of Lake Michigan. No
longer will I be faced with staring into those
lovely eyes that once danced with amusement,
that now are sadly vacant. Her face is so
changed. I never knew how much a difference
a smile made on a person's face, nor did I
know how for granted I took all of the smiles
offered me. Yet, I am not relieved she is gone.
Far from it. Instead I find that every time I
close my own eyes, I feel the squeeze of her
fingers, a goodbye that resonates in me still.
That one last touch, and then nothing. How
was I to know what it signaled? How could I
have guessed what it would portend? My
heavy lids may close for the night, only to be
plagued by visions of her expressionless face,
by her unmoving form. This was a girl whom
I never thought to see at rest, whose perpetual
motion was enough to make me dizzy. How
can this same body be bathed in such eerie
stillness?*

My parents are worried about me. I know this. They hint at returning to school. They dance around the idea of giving her up now that she is so changed. How could I? As if it were possible. I am chained to her, I feel a string from my chest to hers, and the farther she moves away from me, the more that it tugs at my breast.

Sometimes I am angry with her. It is wrong, I know, to be bitter towards a girl who has been shattered beyond recognition. But, I can't help it. I have read all the grisly details, they are in the paper, the police officers read them to Mr. David, I have heard it all. Actions that I cannot even perceive happening. Beyond any power of my imagination, exceeding my wildest nightmares. The stuff of horror stories, truly. But, how could she, Violet, allow that monster of a man and the violence he did her to decide her fate? How could she? Why doesn't she see that her value is in no way diminished, and any person that thinks so isn't human. She is the same girl to me. The same wild, gorgeous, completely wonderful girl that I fell for, all those years ago.

Everyone seems to be asking the same question. Everyone looks to me for the answers. Where will I wander to? Stay here in Chicago, haunted by my own mistakes? Haunted by a thousand happy memories or meaningless tiffs that echo through every step of this urban landscape? No, I cannot. Do I go to her? Do I travel up to the wilderness to watch her dissolve even further into a shadow? Her parents have concocted a plan with the asylum up there, and though I do not know the particulars, I cannot imagine that it will help. And if it would be no help to her or myself, what would be the point? To be tortured daily by the ghost of Violet? Perhaps I should travel, or stay with family in St. Louis.

I am so frustrated! So angry! So powerless. This horrible thing has hit us all, has beaten us soundly so that we are just as dumb to the world as Violet. Some exercise maybe. Some time to clear my mind and think properly. I will think on it, reflect, and then mayhap I will have a clearer vision for where I belong.

Journal

March 1, 1935

What started out as a daily assignment, has become like a visit to an old friend. So, it is with the attitude of confiding in a familiar companion that I find myself coming back once again, to this journal. I have re-read the words in here many times in the past week, and the entries have at different times brought me laughter and tears, and sometimes both in the same moment.

The date alone shows that there was a disturbance in my life from the last time I found myself scratching away at this tome, and what a change. Where to begin? What happened when I made my 'escape'? It is a question that has been on my mind from the moment I first scurried off of the the asylum lands, to the moment I found myself staring into the water. For that moment was a punch in the gut.

I had dressed warmly, and managed somehow to keep my excitement under control, mostly, at least. I left after breakfast. Knowing that the rest of the patients were being attended to, and taking advantage of the more relaxed way I had been looked after the past few weeks, I simply dressed and left. It is always incredible to me, what can be achieved by someone who acts as if they know what they are doing, and carries it off with a complete indifference to those who might see them. So, I simply walked out the door, walked out of the yard, and kept on walking. I knew that if I kept heading north I would run into the water. And I did. Through the trees, making sure to stay well away from any streets. Through my exertions and the warmth of my coat and scarves I had begun to fall victim to that terrible annoyance of cold weather, the core of your body becoming so overheated that you perspire, and my extremities still nipped with the icy flame of cold. I reached into the back collar of my coat and pulled my hair out and up to allow a little of the cold air to enter in. It was such a relief to feel the cool air rushing in. I stopped briefly and looked about me. Evergreens and snowy woods. My hair had fallen all around me, nearly a veil of gold in my eyes. I took in large gulps of air, as if surfacing after almost drowning. *I was out.* I really had no idea of what my plan was now that I had made my escape, but I pushed the doubts, questions and fears to the back of my mind and briskly placed one boot in front of the other on my solitary march to the water's edge.

As soon as the water came in sight, I could think of nothing else. To be near that water was to be connected to everything that had once made sense. As if it could wash away the mysteries that enshrouded me, and somehow make me whole again. Was this really possible? I had to believe it could be. If I'm being honest, though, and there's no reason why I should lie to myself, I wasn't thinking of anything. Simply floating towards the water, all reflection on the meaning of these events has come later, after having lived through them. We always see clearer through the glasses that look backward.

It was colder by the water, and my hair was lifted up and tousled by the wind coming off the lake. The icy caress of nature, assuring me that I had truly come to the right place. I gazed off into the distance, and saw grey blue glass. It wasn't ice, just still. It was strange with the wind blowing for the lake to be so still, but it matched my mood, and I half convinced myself that the water was performing on my behalf. I crouched down, hardly feeling the cold anymore, and after searching the area for a moment, my eyes locked on a dark grey stone, a little larger than the others around it. Picking it up in my gloved hands, I began to chip away at the water. Mindlessly at first, desiring a connection with the lake, I started chipping into the very thin brittle ice, that seemed more than happy to be free to warm and move again as it was in the deeper parts of the water. I began to stand up, with the thought being to toss the stone out, to create ripples in the world from my actions. To create a stir in the world again, after being shut away for so long.

But... I could not stand up. I had seen something in the water. Something strange. A presence. An apparition. I looked back at the space I had flaked away, and saw nothing. Thinking it must be nerves, I made to stand up yet again, when out of the corner of my eye, I saw it again. Feeling truly haunted by this time, I was too curious not to look deeper and settle for myself what I was seeing. A cloud passed over the sun, and in the slightly more darkened pool of water below me, I saw, Violet. Violet's face. Violet's hair. There was a line, a scar on her chin, and she looked weary and more haggard than I had ever seen her. She seemed just as confused and upset to see me. Then, I raised my hand up to my chin and felt the faint line. It extended from the middle of my chin, underneath and back towards my ear. And then I remembered the jarring pain that had written it into my face. I bent so close to the water that I was almost touching it, depending on the shift of the light I could and could not see the image, I noticed that Violet, the image, the apparition.... *I* was crying. I sat back, onto my bottom, no longer peering at the reflection in the water. I was Violet. Violet David. The girl I had admired and felt so close to, whose life I was jealous of, was me. And yet not. I could never be her again.

The day came back to me like the cut of a thousand knives, the hot rancid breath of the man, the echo of his footfalls behind me in the street. I had heard him. I remembered. I had heard the steps, and I had decided that I would brazen it out. Could anyone resist my charm? There was nothing I couldn't talk my way out of, right? How wrong I had been. How foolish. I was so filled with my triumph with Luke. Comfortable with the knowledge that whatever dalliance he'd had with that disgusting necker of a girl was irrefutably over. He was mine and I was his and we were going to take the world by storm.

I felt myself rocking back and forth on the beach, the truths, the memories of my reality slamming into me, gunshots to my stomach. He had slugged me. The way that you see men hit each other in the pictures. I might not have understood the man's words, but when he pushed me into that alleyway, I knew what he wanted. I struggled against him. I spit and yowled like a trapped cat, and I felt that I was about as strong as one against the brute force of his body. He wasn't a large man, not even so tall or muscled as Luke, but it was as if his body had been taken over by an impetus or momentum that was larger than himself. I had never known the fear of being physically powerless before. How can I explain what it is like to experience that kind of fear? You become more of an animal than human when that icy cold terror hits your heart. Could I run? Was I going to die? These aren't even coherent thoughts, just vague feelings, stabs of panic. To look into someone else's eyes and know that they are bent on hurting you. They *wish* to cause you pain. It is indescribable. How can I put into words the kind of fear that wrenches your heart open, bleeding dread on the inside? After the fear and the fight though, there is a feeling of acceptance. Not of consent, no. They cannot be confused. Your body accepts that it can fight no more. It has been beaten, and it is now fighting to survive. It's as if your mind exits for a while, waiting for a time until it is ready to fight again.

After that, I remember very little. Ins and outs, the awful pain searing through my head and traveling all over my body, his rude heaviness on top of me, the hatefulness of what he was doing seeped from his every pore, it permeated his entire being until he became *hate*. The last blow had put me out, and I remembered nothing until the hospital.

Vaguely, my mother's voice. In it was a note of such pain that I shut my eyes to it. My father, steady, the Oak of the family. No matter how the wind blew around our family, he stayed firmly rooted, holding us all in place. But Luke, Luke was there. He was touching my hair, he was reading to me. Caressing my hand. It was for him. I knew, then that the girl they had known, the tempestuous, impulsive, brat-Violet David, was gone. I would never be her again. I would always be broken and pitiful. I would always be an object of sympathy. My attacker may not have killed my body, but he had killed me nonetheless. So I had said goodbye to them. I journeyed into myself, in hiding, allowing myself to be an observer, a friend of the fire that I had once been.

The funny thing about fire, is that it is tempered, controlled by water. And as I sat there, by the water that day, remembering, I realized that I may not be the Violet David of the past, but I could be a new version of myself in the future. I was me. No matter what happened to me, no matter how many times my flames went out, no matter how much they were stomped on, it was up to me to re-light them. I would do it.

Luke's words came back to me. He had said that the he would always love Violet, but that he had room in his heart for me too. At least that's what I had hoped he meant. I saw, that he was admitting I wasn't the same, but letting the me that I had hidden inside know, that he loved any version of myself that I chose. So what would I do? What was my choice? Would I be well? Or, although part of me would always be gone, a piece of me would never be quite alive, I could still choose to forge a new me. A stronger, more resilient woman. A woman who could not and would not let her fate be decided for her. I would seize the thread of my own life, and measure it myself, and I would not allow it to be cut until I was done with it.

I filled with peace. The peace of resolve, the peace that deciding on an action brings. I followed my feet up from the water, through the snowy little town and fairly danced up to our lake house doorstep. I was home, everyone who had ever mattered was behind that door, and I would no longer allow it to be shut between us anymore.

I shook out my hair, letting it cascade down the front of my shoulders, I pinched my cheeks, and adding that feline grin that felt so right on my face, I lifted my knuckles to rap on the door. Before I even had an opportunity to let the sound of my homecoming resonate through the house, I felt a warm breath on my hair, a soft embrace around my waist, I looked down at the hand that was lightly holding my midsection, and saw the ruddy fingers tinged with cold, the sleeves of his peacoat unmistakable. I turned around to face Luke, his grey-green eyes, stared straight into mine, and he said,

"It's about time, Violet. Cash or check?"

AFTERWORD

Rape and attacks on women in the 1930s were viewed much differently than they are today. Many rapes were not reported on, and the police in most cases took little notice of them. There were exceptions, but, by and large, rape then, as it still is today to a slightly lesser extent, was a source of shame to the victim. There was very little emphasis on the plights victims at all back then, with much more interest in suspects, especially if the crimes crossed racial lines.

As far as the asylum, it is a real place that has always haunted me. It is near my father's house in Traverse City, MI and is in the process of being renovated. Many of the buildings have been converted into charming lofts, restaurants, and shops. There are still others though, that seem to carry an eerie sadness with them still. The first time I brought my husband to see the gorgeous old buildings, before I had even told him what it used to be, he remarked that the place gave him the chills, and that he imagined "some very sad things had happened here". It was an interesting thought. Could a place harbor the feelings of those who had lived there? Could they leech into the walls of a building and become as tangible as the building itself? Perhaps.

Upon further research into the hospital, I found a lot of information about the uses for different buildings, and the types of patients that lived there. The asylum itself operated from 1885 to 1989, and over the years there were many additions and changes to the way the building was used and the types of treatments administered. In the early 1930s, when this book is set, lobotomies were first being introduced to the world of psychotherapy.

In the story, Violet is suffering from symptoms that are most closely resembling a disassociation with reality, she has in fact created a new identity for herself because the violence done to her was too much for her to accept or process. The behavior she exhibits would most closely be described as schizophrenic, but as I am not a licensed psychologist, I would not presume to diagnose her.

Traverse City, now a bustling vacation escape, was very different in the early part of the 20th century. Much of the town's economy had relied on timber, and on the local orchards for producing cherries and apples. Traverse City is still known for its cherries, and holds a festival every year in July. I have described the city as a "wilderness" many times throughout this book, and it is both to affect the imagination of the reader, and to reflect the attitude of the characters. Traverse City of this time period may not have been wilderness in the strictest sense, but to a family recently removed from the Metropolis of Chicago, it would have been an apt description.

Similar to Violet, I myself have always felt a pull to the water of Lake Michigan. It does seem to have a calming, healing effect. There is something about the way the wind blows overhead, and the simplicity of a summer day in Northern Michigan, that awakens one differently than any other shoreline.

If you'd like to read more on rape in the 30s, or any time in recent American History, I would suggest, Helen Benedict's *Virgin or Vamp: How the Press Covers Sex Crimes*. For more information on the history of the Traverse City State Hospital, I would highly recommend Chris Miller's *Traverse City State Hospital*.

ALEXANDRIA NOLAN

SHEARS OF FATE

ABOUT THE AUTHOR

Alexandria Nolan was born and raised in Flint, Michigan. She attended the University of Michigan-Flint, and graduated with a degree in English. After teaching elementary, middle and high school English and History she turned back to her first love--writing. She is the author of "Paradise of Exiles" a travel memoir of the Amalfi Coast, and is currently working on a collection of short stories.

Other writings include *Greetings from Nolandia*, a lifestyle and travel blog, and various contributions to print and online media.

She currently lives in Houston, Texas with her husband, Terrence, and an assortment of rescued pets. When not writing she can be found yoga-ing, reading or traveling.

greetingsfromnolandia.com

32241330R00101

Made in the USA
Charleston, SC
12 August 2014